Perilous Kinship

Perilous Kinship

Zafer Şenocak

Translated by Tom Cheesman

Hafan Books   Swansea

Hafan Books

c/o Tom Cheesman, School of Arts,
Swansea University, Wales, SA2 8PP

www.hafan.org   07736408064

t.cheesman@swansea.ac.uk

All proceeds to Swansea Bay Asylum Seekers Support Group

First published as *Gefährliche Verwandtschaft*,
Babel Verlag, Munich, 1998

Text © Zafer Şenocak, 1998
Translation © Tom Cheesman, 2001–9

Front cover: "Central Powers negotiators at Brest-Litovsk, Dec. 1917: Gen. Hoffmann
(Germany), Ottokar Czernin (Austria-Hungary), Talaat Pasha (Ottoman Empire),
Richard v. Kühlmann (Germany)" – from www.histdoc.net/historia/1917-
18/brest1.html

Back cover: from www.citirealty.net/photo/100_2259.jpg

Out of Line series # 9B

Design: TC

Printed by Lulu.com

Order from: www.lulu.com/hafan

ISBN 978-0-9562409-4-1

Remembering is telling without words.

Sumerian saying

There are words under the tongue that tell nothing.
They are not even good for asking questions.
They remember.

Levantine wisdom

1

When I woke up, where the bullet had hit my face I had a spot. It was only a little inflamed, so I didn't notice it until I touched it when I was shaving. I don't wet-shave, so there was no blood, just a dull pain that reminded me of the pain I had woken up with.

I don't know why I was in the bus that was attacked. I don't know where I was going. I don't even know where I was. I often use public transport, since I have no car. But the bus was different from the yellow double-deckers in my city. Unless I am mistaken, it was blue, and not very full. I had sat down in the back row, as I always do. In my opinion that's where you get the best road feel. Besides, the front rows of seats are usually the ones that take the damage in an accident.

When they fired into the bus from outside, no one was hit. People ducked. They stayed calm; seemed to be used to such incidents, as if there was nothing special about life being on the line.

Inside the bus all was calm. No one moved. I noticed that the bus had no driver. A man with a machine-gun came aboard through the door at the front. He pointed the weapon at me and began firing. I ducked slightly, so he hit me in the head. This is normally fatal. But instead of dying, I woke up. The first thing I noticed was how tidy the room was.

I was in an expensive hotel. I don't know why I had such a bad dream in this hotel last night. The whole city reminded me of an expensive hotel. Like the better kind of hotels, cities too are becoming more and more alike. The notary had arranged everything here for me.

"A room for two nights, in case there should be complications," the friendly voice on the phone had said, audibly concerned to dispel suspicion.

"Complications?"

"That depends entirely on you. If you don't have any queries it will all be very quick. The hotel is very close to the chancery."

I had arranged to meet an old school friend for dinner, in an Italian restaurant on the right bank of the Isar. I walked. It was half-dark. The sun had just gone down and the street lights weren't yet on. The houses were old and beautiful and struck me as carefree. How melancholy Berlin was, compared to this gay city in the south. Childhood feelings welled up. This was the city where my mother had given birth to me. Though I had been conceived somewhere quite different. In a far bigger and older city, in the south east, on the edge of Europe. Maybe my parents chose this city, when they came to Germany, because it was in the south east, near the border. It had the charm of all border-towns: not too big, but ambitious. People here were proud of constantly proving the following to the rest of the world: we brew the best beer, we make the fastest cars, and we have the lowest crime rates. A city with an attitude and a programme like this will get rich quickly. The natives were accustomed to living with strangers. It was a good place to come to, people felt like natives in a matter of days. It was not uncommon for incomers, as they were usually called here, to be instructing natives in local matters after no more than a brief acclimatisation. Such importunity was punished by using the local dialect, mastery of which could only be acquired through drinking the milk of a native mother.

I would have liked most of all to take the tram to Grünewald, where my mother's father owned a small house, our house. But time was short. The family called it 'the cottage', although its smart location in Grünewald made it quite valuable.

The Nazis had used it as a Hitler Youth hang-out. I grew up in this house. I loved playing in the storage space under the roof, because the garden was too dangerous. There were thought to be mines buried in it. One day, in a dusty box underneath a pile of tools, I found a series of photos. They all showed a man with a funny moustache. When I showed the photos to my parents, they were immediately burned in the fireplace.

The notary has been reading for half an hour. He reads in a monotone, his voice is sending me to sleep. I stopped listening some time ago. In a golden dish on his very tidy desk are scissors of various sizes. They remind me of the objects on my own desk. Next to the scissors is a silver box.

2

Grandfather had left only a short farewell letter. When, following the death of my parents, who had been divorced for years but had died in a road accident in the same car, I received from the notary the silver box which had once been my grandfather's, I was surprised how heavy it was. The silver had been damaged in several places. The box was about the size of a stack of three telephone directories, and looked mysterious.

"Does it have a key?" I asked. The notary raised his head from his papers and said only: "It's open."

I left the notary without opening the box. He had not asked me to. There could not be anything special in it, certainly nothing valuable. It would have been mentioned in the list of effects. I was the sole heir. I had inherited the house in Grünewald, several flats and cars, as well as a fair amount in shares. There was a trustee, so all I had to do was sign the necessary documents and give my account number. I had received regular bank transfers from my father. I had never really had any financial difficulties. There were some less good times, but they were more due to my poor housekeeping than to any shortage of money. Sometimes I also lent money to friends. I never saw it again. I didn't mind. In this country, where I was born and grew up, money is at the centre of everything, true, but one behaves as if all these things with money at their centre were unimportant. If one has no money, one simply does not belong. And if one has money, one needn't give a damn about anything. Not even about money. Which is why the intelligent immigrants in this country care not about such worthless things as German nationality, or the German passport, but first and foremost about the German mark. For that alone decides the question of belonging, which in Germany is a question of existence.

It was completely different in my grandfather's country. There too, money governed all human relations. But there was no shortage of it. Expressed in figures, there was far more money than anywhere in the world. But it was worth nothing. And because it was losing value daily, it had become the only subject people talked about. It is odd that money becomes the more important, the less it is worth. As the value of their money diminished, one could see the people's self-confidence diminishing too.

This impression struck me even on my short visits, which had more to do with tourism than with family. And already by the second day I was behaving like all the others. Leaving my hotel in the morning, the first thing I did was to visit the bureau de change and check the Turkish lira against the dollar and the German mark on the electronic displays.

After seeing the notary I flew back to Berlin the same day. I could not imagine spending another night in the room where I had had that strange dream. I was home again. I was alone. Marie was out, as so often, doing research in the State Library. She rarely came home before nine. I stood the silver box on the kitchen table. It looked good there. I took a damp cloth and wiped the box. Whenever I come home, I always go into the kitchen first. The kitchen is the room nearest the front door. Also that is where my favourite sofa is, dark red, torn, with curved arm-rests. A messenger from the last century.

I made a pot of coffee. It was five in the afternoon, getting dark outside already. Winter days in this city are short. They seem even shorter because the sky seldom clears all day. It usually stays grey. Fog lies upon the city, swallowing first the houses, then the people.

With the coffee running through the machine I went decisively over to the box and slid the bolt on the lock. It was a little rusty and resisted being opened. Dust spilled towards me. Inside were notebooks in a neat pile. I lifted one of the books and leafed through it. It was full of writing in Arabic and in places also Cyrillic script. Cyrillic letters were an early experience of foreignness for me, seen on the long journeys by car and train through the Balkans. They started appearing beyond an invisible border where one left our culture. A script is learned in order to master the world. It must be a hard blow indeed to find one's own script is suddenly worth nothing. I never learned Turkish properly. I just know a few words. No more than the average German tourist.

All the notebooks, apart from the last, were full. There were twenty altogether. All of the same French kind with grey cardboard covers. They were numbered by year, beginning in 1916 and ending in 1936. I had learned Arabic numerals as a child, when I was keen on maths. "Our numbers come from the Arabs," my father declared. I protested out loud. Surely that could not be true. The Arabs were even poorer than the Turks. "A long time ago it was very different," my father replied. I still did not want to believe it. The next day he presented me with an Arabic alphabet, which long fascinated me, though I learned little from it. I only know how to write the numbers.

If these really were grandfather's diaries I was holding in my hands, he must have been a very pedantic man. Not one word was crossed out. Every entry was roughly the same length. There seemed to be a page for each day. The handwriting was regular and looked very beautiful. I must have been leafing through the notebooks for hours when I heard the door open and Marie came in.

Marie is tired. She asks if there is anything to eat.

"Oh, I completely forgot you were in Munich. How was it?"

Before I can say anything she notices the notebooks on the table and leafs through them for a while, fascinated.

"Maybe now you can solve a few puzzles," she murmurs, then gives me a challenging look.

"I don't want to solve any puzzles," I answer weakly. "Let's go out to eat."

We go to the Greek on the corner. Marie talks.

"We got some footage in Hardenberg Strasse today. More or less exactly where Talat Pasha was shot by that young Armenian. The cameramen were very impatient because of the cold. I don't know if there's any point going back to the place where it happened seventy years after, to try and capture something. If I'd found witnesses from back then still alive, we could have got them there saying something. But this is just getting silent pictures. Rather a dull place, lots of young people about. It could be footage for a film about Berlin after the Wall. We'd just finished when another camera crew turned up to shoot on exactly the same spot. I got a shock. I was relieved when it was just a French team making a documentary about the Technical University. Have you finished that book about the Young Turks yet? Did you find out anything new about Talat Pasha? Or maybe his wife? I don't suppose you did. How many wives did he have, actually?"

"Must you always orientalise? With this kind of hostility, how do you expect to make an interesting documentary about the man?"

"Should I feel sympathy for a mass murderer? I'm allowed not to love Hitler, aren't I."

"But that's completely different."

"Oh really? Why?"

"The issue's not what you're allowed or not allowed. You're making a film about a controversial historical figure, you have to be able to adopt different perspectives."

"My perspective is enough for me."

"So why are you getting me to read as many different sources as possible for you? Have you made any effort to find Turkish sources for example, which probably give a completely different picture of events and personalities from the western sources. There's not a single biography of Talat in a western language. Which shows how one-sidedly history is written. They've made the Armenians, that deeply oriental people, into fictional westerners, just because they lived as Christians in a Moslem environment. But the Turks, the most western oriented people in the region, are never going to be accepted by the Europeans as such, because they're Moslems."

"You're starting to sound like a Turkish politician. You'll have to abolish torture if you want to become Europeans."

"So were the French not Europeans when they were torturing and killing in Algeria? Or the English, when they were plundering half the world? Were they excluded from the Council of Europe for that, or from the EEC? You Europeans play false, your tongue is forked. White man speak always with forked tongue."

I loved this line of Winnetou's so much that I had completely forgotten that the woman sitting across from me was my wife. Marie said nothing, picked at her food with her fork. We had hardly eaten. The waitress, who knew us well, came over to ask if she should warm the food up for us again. We declined.

Marie and I usually cleared the bad atmosphere after such disagreements by going to bed. That night too we did not forgo our love play, although we were both very tired. It was shorter than usual, but intensive.

Sometimes, when I was sitting working at my desk facing the window, Marie would undress, come up behind me and put her arms around me. I liked her to take possession of me like that. I would close my eyes and concentrate on the feel of her breath on my neck. I could feel my stillness intensifying her desire. I would open my eyes and see her hands. Marie had beautiful, calm hands.

Marie and I held tightly to one another, partly perhaps because we disliked company. We liked being one in our self-sufficient pairdom.

3

I had met Marie in America. We had gone back to Berlin together, hoping to find a permanent home in this city. At least, that had been my hope. I had left West Berlin in February 1989, to put distance between myself and the wreck of a relationship. A further reason was that my first book of stories, "Veronika – Report on a Contemporary Love", had not been a success. The few reviews which appeared were unable to make anything of this admittedly cliché-ridden love story. Only one obscure magazine, with the title "The Eighties – A Journal for Love and Crime", published a very long analysis of the book, which I judged to be a positive review, having read it several times and still not managed to understand it. We are like guests in this world. I do not mean this in the worn-out mystical sense. I mean it literally. In the course of every visit a point comes when one feels it is time to go. If one misses this moment, things become problematic. One's hosts try to persuade one to stay the night. The last Underground train has gone, topics of conversation run out. One has too much to drink, finds oneself in an uncomfortable bed, can be confident of never being invited back again. I did not want to be an uninvited guest in Berlin, nor to become a tolerated long-term guest.

A small college in America had offered me a post as writer in residence. This offer came at exactly the right time. I could be confident that nobody knew me there, apart from the three people in the German department. I chose the seclusion of the American prairie in order to capture new impressions and think about my future. Berlin was a wounded but peaceful city then. It was not a particularly hard city to leave. Many people here were living out of removals crates. In any case I had never had my own flat in Berlin, just a series of rooms. When I was away travelling, I usually sub-let my room. In order to make the leap irreversible, when I left for America I gave up my room completely. It was rented by a young couple who had just crossed over from the East, and only wanted to use Berlin as a springboard for an existence in West Germany.

I stayed longer in America than planned. If Marie had not turned up where I was living snowbound for six months of the year, I might never have come back. When we arrived in Berlin in the summer of 1992, superficially almost nothing had changed. True, the border controls had gone, one could go freely to East Berlin. But nobody forced one to do so. I was surprised that everyone in the city was talking about change, although little had changed. I believe it was a longing for change, mingled with fear, which made change a topic of conversation: after three years in America I had to get used once again to the fact that unreal things are worth just as much in Germany as real ones.

Marie was a Berliner. She had been born in this city and her parents too, with whom she refused to have any contact, because they voted Christian Democrat, were genuine Berliners. Her father's family were of Huguenot background, her mother's from Silesia. From the first moment I saw her, I felt that this nondescript, flat-chested, always rather pale-looking woman could help me in my search for a homeland. She was a person whose life had a clear focus, enabling her to be the same far away as she was at home. Whereas I, far away, felt naked. I had the feeling that I had to get a new set of clothes. After we had decided to combine our life-paths, Marie made all the decisions. I had no doubts that these decisions would be to my advantage too.

Marie was a language teacher who was obsessed with words. All the more surprising to me was her decision to apply to study at the Film Academy in Berlin.

But she saw no contradiction in this.

"Images are only words too," was her pithy comment. "One just has to be willing to read them. Do you know the difference between looking and seeing? To see an image is by no means to know how to read it. Only those who look can read."

more meaningless. It just fills a pause in the conversation.

"There are a couple of things I must say to you. We see each other so seldom. And I'm not as young as I was. Today might be the last time we see each other. When I die, I want you to inherit not only money, which I still have enough of, but also a couple of secrets I've carried with me all my life. I've never known anyone I could entrust them to. Those closest to me were just the same as the strangers who wanted to get close to me, thinking it'd be to their advantage. I took off to be free of them. Only you are still close to me. A son is still a son, especially when he's the only one."

Father still has long to live, goes through my mind. I do not feel close to him. What will his death mean to me? I pull myself together and try to seem interested. But I cannot disguise my surprise. Secrets, a kind of testament, all without the presence of a notary, under the roof of a five star hotel, in a city I'd always found mysterious.

"I'm living here because I've discovered that this is the best place to hide. It's a city of people who've gone underground, like New York or Hong Kong in this respect. Cities like Singapore or Peking betray one immediately, especially a foreigner like me. One is not in a familiar environment. It's different here. I still know every nook and cranny. This European part of the city is where I grew up. I'm a child of the Republic after all, I was born in the same year." He smiles. "I still remember the parades on Taksim Square on the anniversaries of the Republic. The square was full of flags and young people. It was much prettier then. The old houses have disappeared, leaving their shadows behind like stage sets that only I can see. They block the view of the ugly new buildings, keep the familiar atmosphere intact."

"What are you hiding from? From a lover? Something to do with business? Terrorists?"

"No, it's impossible to hide from terrorists here. If they really want someone they'll catch him. But my body's worth nothing to them, and as for what's in my head, they know nothing about it. People in this country always underestimate the value of knowledge. They only believe in what they can see, smell or taste. There aren't even any usable directories. The newest phone books are ten years old."

"We're not here to talk about the problems of Turkey, are we?" I interrupt.

"No, you're right, I've no need to tell you about that. But one more thing, your grandfather hid in this city too. For two years, 1919 to 1921, he lived in a miserable cottage on the hills of Üsküdar. He pretended to be a member of a pious order whose job was taking care of simple things for the brethren. Nobody thought he was a driven, power-obsessed opportunist or a national hero, since he was a bit of everything and supremely skilled at hiding one feature of his character behind another." He stops, looks at me thoughtfully. "These days I can't stop dreaming about my father. Perhaps these dreams are letting me have some of the life I could not share with him. When he died I was only thirteen, you see."

"Tell me something about your life now. What do you do all day? Do you have a lover? Do you still gamble? How much money's left in your account? Oh, what business is that of mine."

"Sometimes I go for walks in the city. I walk aimlessly through the streets, letting the crowds propel me. In the afternoons I visit a coffee-house. A different one each time, so nobody talks to me. In the evenings I stay in my hotel room, watching television, or listening to the German world service on my short wave radio. The reception on short wave is especially good. I've made some good money on the stock exchange here, by the way. If you keep your eyes and ears open here, you can make a good fast buck. In six months I made almost as much as I spent in the last ten years, and I wasn't living like a monk."

We have finished our drinks and leave. In the lift I shut my eyes and wonder if I should say goodbye downstairs. I could visit a couple of friends this evening, people I've not seen for ages. Will their phone numbers still work? Do people here still move as often as they used to? Or have the nomads settled down at last, reconciled to growing old in large stone buildings?

Outside the hotel we get in a taxi and drive down the steep hill. "You don't have a car?" He shakes his head. As far back as I can remember, father always drove big American cars. For me that associated him with films. Between the trees the sea can be seen.

"So you were here all summer?"

"I came in May, just like Mehmet the Conqueror. One should always come to Istanbul in May if one wants to be made welcome. It'll be time to say goodbye soon, though I've no destination in mind yet. Actually, there isn't a more exciting stock exchange anywhere at the moment."

The taxi stops outside brightly lit fruit stalls. I recognize Beşiktaş market. Further back is the fish market. In brightly coloured plastic buckets, freshly caught fish thrash in the water. Bigger ones lie motionless on straw among small bits of ice.

"You still like to eat fish?"

I nod. We push our way across the quayside through the crowds and enter a restaurant on the seafront. We sit at a small table by a window with steamed-up panes. The owner brings a jug of warm white wine. He exchanges glances with father.

"I come here sometimes. You know I used to like fishing. It doesn't get so crowded here as other places. The people aren't so horribly ill-mannered. One doesn't see mobile phones on the tables, and not many women with dyed blonde hair."

That is all I can remember, not even our parting.

5

So grandfather had lived underground in Istanbul for two years.

I look in the notebooks from 1919 and 1920. They are scarcely different from the others. The writing is no hastier, nor are the books themselves different. They seem neither newer nor older. But does a man living under a false identity keep a diary?

When the Ottoman Empire entered the First World War on the German side, grandfather had just turned 19. A good age to go into battle.

In 1919, when he was 23, the empire which had once stretched over three continents lay in ruins. Grandfather was among those who did not give up. He was one of the many who gathered around the 'Great Saviour' Mustafa Kemal. He spied for his army in Istanbul while the city was under occupation by the victorious powers. In 1921 he went to Anatolia to fight the Greeks on the western front. At the front he met my grandmother Hatice, a determined young woman. She came from a wealthy merchant family in Istanbul, and had had an Islamic upbringing which in no way stifled her militant nature. Hatice, who spoke fluent Greek, was a spy too. Her relationship with grandfather was battle-tested. The war was still in progress, the Turkish armies had yet to achieve their final victory, when they were married. The 'Great Saviour' was their witness at the ceremony.

How should one picture the 'Great Saviour' now? Every profession which has to be practised with authority is in crisis. Even in aeroplanes, control has been transferred to computers. It seems to me that a Great Saviour would destroy a people sooner than save it.

The Great Saviour was an art-loving man. He loved art because he wanted to civilize his people. He loved the theatre since it was the most civilized art form. A civilization with no theatre was like a bathroom with no mirror. Cultures which had no theatre or did not hold theatre in high regard had produced no high civilization, in the Great Saviour's view. The example he gave was the Arabs, sons of the desert as he called them. The Arabs had wasted their theatrical talent in the form of mere poetry. They were incapable of capturing the fire of their feelings in language.

From the beginning of his reign of absolute power it had been the Great Saviour's habit to proof-read every play performed at the state theatre before rehearsals began. More than once it happened that plays by Molière or Shakespeare received a final polish from his hand, a hand that had not only proved its skill in the total annihilation of enemies in war, but also seemed to have the necessary feel for controlling language.

If the Great Saviour's intention was to civilize his people, this had to mean that the people was uncivilized until his time. To be civilized was to eat sitting at a table and using cutlery. The uncivilized sat on the ground and ate with their hands. The lavatories of the civilized too were different from the natives'. This was an alarming signal. For a while it had even been feared that everyone would have to relearn how to relieve themselves. But the body and its limitations make a person everywhere the same. In view of the numberless mental differences between people, this is reassuring.

I don't know why the Great Saviour never wrote a play of his own. Maybe he died too soon. But maybe too, the executors of his estate have been doing a sloppy job.

Instead of writing a play the Great Saviour made rather a long speech. This was a mistake. He was not a great speaker. He spoke in a high, trembling voice, in chopped-up periods, swallowing syllables. The Great Saviour had succeeded in saving his people, but not in civilizing them.

6

In America I had happened to be in one of the few colleges where the German department did not admire the East German workers' and peasants' republic. Adenauer was held in high esteem, Schiller and Goethe were studied, and the keenly read contemporary authors were dissidents like Reiner Kunze, and of course Ernst Jünger, in many eyes a gateway to understanding eternal Germanness, whose works were passed around like keys to the truth. Brecht and Grass were disliked. My attempts to read Böll with the students met with considerable scepticism. "Didn't he support the terrorists?" one colleague asked suspiciously.

When I came back to Berlin from America I was astonished at the mood in Berlin. The Wall had gone, and in the very next moment a new, united Germany had emerged, not some loose federation of regional states but a proper German nation-state. Yet every day the numbers of those who wished the Wall would come back were growing. I could understand the ones who had lost their jobs after the 'turn', or those who were too stiff-jointed to make the political 'turn' themselves. They had lost something and were grieving for the old days, which now seemed in hindsight like the days of a secure childhood. For believing subjects, the end of a dictatorship can mean something like the loss of a beloved father. But in my circles I also met rather left-wing contemporaries from the west who had been seized by an inexplicable disquiet. They had suddenly discovered how much they loved their little capital city of Bonn, and they saw a national danger in the great metropolis Berlin becoming the new capital of united Germany. And all in all, this united Germany, wasn't it bound to become a cradle of ill-fortune? Was it not a good thing that the German nation-state had finally been shattered in 1945? Germany was like a courtroom full of non-stop accusing and judging. Where since the 1960s, if not before, it had been the Nazis and their henchmen who had been in the dock, now they were being joined by Stasi agents, informers, functionaries of the former Socialist Unity Party, politicians in general in fact, bogus asylum seekers, the UN, Serbs, professors of peace studies, three-cup-tricksters, Turkish generals, the Kurds, left-wing schoolteachers, neo-Nazis, the ideologists of the 70s and the idlers of the 80s. A nation of court ushers, barristers and judges was being kept fully occupied.

"One often feels one's soul is being operated on, and without any anaesthetic," said an old man I got talking to in the Underground recently. He talked about the fall of the Wall as if his own body had been opened up.

We of negations. Back to back, Germany is going through a sexless union. The strongest part of a German's body is his back, followed by his arm.

Couldn't the GDR have simply joined the EU as a democratic but sovereign state, like Austria? A German 'nation' seemed like Pandora's box to many people. It had been kept locked shut for long years. And now suddenly one was supposed to feel one was a German again. Even if one was not a professional historian. One would have liked to have had a chance to discuss these things at slightly greater length. But the chancellor had foiled everybody's game-plans. The very man one had mocked as the wait-and-see-er and putter-off of decisions, and whose generous bodily bulk gave every reason to expect a certain slowness. This man had simply stretched out his arm and plucked the ripe apple from the tree of history. I was impressed. And evidently I was not alone. A couple of friends from the east of the city, on the radical left as I had always thought, who found Honecker's communism insufficiently authentic, had voted Christian Democrat in the first free elections. They were quite open about this and called the CDU 'the party of the moment'. Had they not got into a fury a few years before when Honecker was making deals with the fascistic Bavarian Franz-Josef Strauss in order to get hard currency credits? As promised, chancellor Kohl brought the D-mark to the east. I began to understand that money was more important for other people than it was for me. I was an heir and did not even need to work. I had a certain amount transferred every month from the interest on my wealth and carried on living modestly, but lacking nothing. Hardly anyone knew I was wealthy.

7

I am told people are astonished how quickly I got over my parents' sudden death. I am accustomed to passing over the rare painful moments in my life in silence. There is no strategy in this. It is just a reaction to my awkwardness in the face of pain and a deeply felt distaste for any kind of fetishistic treatment of suffering.

I have seldom imagined my parents together. Whereas my mother was always with me, my father was often absent. I always had to seek him out in order to be with him. So I find it very difficult to picture them dying together. I had had nothing to do with my parents for a long time. Their sudden death left no gaps in my life, nor did I find myself feeling a sense of loss. For they will not disappear from my thoughts even in the future.

My father had never liked to talk about the past. At least, not to tell stories. "In stories all riddles are solved," he claimed. "And for secrets we have no language." For a long time I had no interest in knowing what secrets he had. Whether or not he wanted to entrust them to me. Why should a man who cannot even communicate with his wife confide in his son? I had got used to reading my father's eyes. The eyes provide a means of access to any closed face. All her life my mother had neglected to look into my father's eyes. Yet one look could have saved her asking all the questions that drove my father away.

They were on the way to Munich when the accident happened. I imagine them on the way to an empty house somewhere on the edge of the city. Perhaps they needed the desolation of an uninhabited house to find each other again. They intended to renovate this house together, make it habitable, make it their dwelling. They intended to be together again in their old age, to overcome the distance between them which no longer meant freedom, as it once had, but loneliness, which they feared most of all. Or they were just driving to see the notary in order to settle a couple of details concerning the will. After concluding the formalities they would have parted as soon as they were outside the notary's door, politely and formally, like two experienced business partners, perhaps afterwards they would also have gone for a meal together and after a couple of hours of relaxed companionship they would have parted again, going off in different directions.

8

I could have regarded grandfather's notebooks simply as part of my collection of manuscripts. With their ornate script they would have occupied an exotic place in this collection. I did not keep them in the boxes I had acquired to house my collection, however, but in one of the large drawers in my desk. They were safe in the silver box where in all likelihood my grandfather had placed them. Sometimes, on days when nothing came to me for my own manuscripts, I fetched them out of their hiding place and leafed through them for a while, until I was overcome by an irresistible tiredness. It is always tiring to look for any length of time at a script one cannot read.

I had long since decided not to reconstruct my grandfather's life but to invent it.

I had information about him I was trying to forget. Should I destroy his diaries in order to liberate my memory completely? Were they not part of my memory, even though I could not read them? I was unable to answer these questions until I had invented the character of my grandfather. I believed that the years 1908 to 1914 had shaped my grandfather's personality. His generation stood with one foot in the Ottoman Empire, the other in the Republic, called upon to connect the end and the beginning. The question of power had existential significance for this generation. They could not delegate power. They were the men of the ruins who built a new house out of the building stones of a collapsing empire. When they were ready to move into the house, there was hardly anyone there. The people had stayed behind on battlefields.

My generation flees from power. We regard it as unprofitable. We do not struggle. We will give a person who exercises power a visiting card sooner than the coup de grace.

For my part I have decided to write.

When I write, all the organs of my body are set in motion, turning themselves into language. Language is an attempt to escape time.

1915 is the year of corpses. The Ottoman Empire has entered the war on the side of the German Empire.

Grandfather at age nineteen. He is in Kars, where he was born. He is an agent behind the front line. He speaks perfect Armenian and Russian and has pale skin. "You're like three men." The commander sends him to scout.

Grandfather did not want to be an Ottoman. But what then was he? A man with a bowler hat and an umbrella and a fountain pen he wrote with. Would he have liked to be an Englishman, or a German? Who or what one is one cannot choose, it is decided by the others, those who do not count one as one of them. Anyone who once in his life tries to change sides learns this.

Marie is collecting facts for her film. Old documents, photos, witness statements. Worthless things in my view. For my part I have decided to write.

I am a grandchild of victims and perpetrators. I do not believe that guilt can be inherited. Not even by the victims from the perpetrators. Guilt sinks into the earth upon which the deed was carried out. There it lies under the feet of the perpetrator. I will tear open the earth beneath my grandfather's feet, shovel him free of his guilt. I must find this spot of earth, unmarked in any atlas.

"The earth," says Marie, "only drinks the blood of the victims, it doesn't bear the guilt of the perpetrators. You'll find nothing if you go there but a run-down border town."

When the word guilt is used in Germany, it is the same as the word for debt, but no one thinks of an overdrawn account. Guilt means genocide. I am interested in murders in general. They are relevant to my work, which lives off people's unpredictability. Aren't we all afraid of our own unpredictability?

Grandfather at age twenty-five. A hero of the east. He is the first to draw up a deportation list of Armenian names. Five hundred names are said to have been on this list. He deletes one name from the list. A woman's name. But why?

Grandfather at age thirty-five. A powerful man. A man whose guilt has made him powerful. A candidate for the office of mayor. His opponent belongs to the same party. The candidate's trick: before the election he distributes left-footed shoes to the voters. After the election they get the matching right-footed shoes. Before the election grandfather sets up a shoe factory. He wins the election.

9

I had reason to doubt that grandfather committed suicide. A man who keeps such a careful record of his life is unlikely to depart it without explaining himself in a final letter, I thought. Or was the final letter hidden in his diaries? I was assuming that these diaries were too intimate for me to give them to someone to have them deciphered. Ought I to learn the languages and scripts he had used myself? I began with the Arabic script, so as to have more time to decide whether I wanted to know who my grandfather was, and what lay behind his death at the age of forty.

Grandfather kept a diary. I write books. A diary is not a book. Rather it is an organ of the one who writes. It reveals what the teller of a story hides from his characters. The crucial question in storytelling is whether the writer, the characters, and the reader, under the spell of the story being told, can find themselves.

10

Perhaps I shouldn't have followed Marie, and from America I shouldn't have gone back to Berlin but to Munich. Alone, without Marie, who was determined to go to Berlin. My best friend lives in Munich. He's a successful businessman who often visits me in Berlin because he is in the area on business. He often travels to eastern Europe and keeps inviting me to accompany me on his trips. Once I spent a week in Riga with him. A beautiful city, its beauty surpassed only by that of its women. Peter was there to meet some American businessmen from Arizona. While he attended his meetings, I roamed through this fascinating, animated city. It resembled a princess who'd woken from a lengthy, imposed sleep, and was preparing herself for her wedding. Painting, restoring, polishing going on everywhere. But no sign of the prince at all. No one even knew exactly who he was or where he came from. On no account could he possibly be a Russian or a Pole. At a pinch, a German. But the Germans had entirely abandoned their monarchist traditions. In every way they were traitors to their history, all in order to please the Americans. They had always thought of history as a parlour game that unites a harmonious family and keeps quarrelsome brothers apart. "One mustn't betray one's own history to strangers," they were saying here. I drove a rented car through the nearby countryside. Nobody there was waiting for a prince, they hadn't even heard of the busy princess.

In the evening I met Peter in a large gathering, and the dominance of the American businessmen, expressed above all in their boisterousness and loudness, almost made me think I was back home in America. I myself was surprised that after spending three years in America I called it my "home". But behind this observation lies a rule. I always call the place where I last lived home. In Berlin I was at home in Munich. Now, after coming back to Berlin, my home is America. To be at home in a place I must have left it at least once.

"I negotiate joint ventures," Peter says, but no one knows exactly what his business is. We have known each other since we were schoolboys. Although I have known him so long, I too suspect that behind his friendly façade there is a second world of impenetrable laws that govern him. His life consists of a chain of contradictions. He is a bohemian and leads a conventional family life. He feels for art and lives for figures. He is generous and can be tough as nails negotiating business deals. He is conservative in his thinking and has been a member of the Social Democrats since he was eighteen. Perhaps it is these contradictions that keep him alive. Everyone balances the contradictions in their life in order to walk upright, but few people show them so openly.

Peter was not born in Munich. His parents came to Bavaria as refugees from Silesia after the Second World War, because Bavaria was a Catholic region. After fleeing, they had spent some weeks near Lippstadt. As soon as they had gathered their strength a little, they fled that Protestant territory. Peter's parents had been married in January 1945. Just one week later they were fleeing from the Russians. They were both 19 then. I have never met a couple who held together so strongly as Peter's parents. It almost seemed they were still fleeing, dependent on one another in body and soul. Like me, Peter was an only child, and we quickly made friends at grammar school. Gertrude, Peter's mother, was soon trying to convince me of the advantages of the Catholic religion, with no success. Nor did she succeed in preventing her son, at eighteen, from joining the Social Democrats, a party run by Protestants.

Now Peter is trying to persuade me to come to Munich and join his company. "Writing will never get you anywhere. It's time you made some money," he says. This directness, which would be deeply wounding coming from anyone else, I do not mind from him. I am used to people intervening in my life in order to improve it.

Driving back from Riga we had lots of time to talk. Due to stormy weather the return flight had been cancelled and Peter rented a fast BMW. He loved these cars. For him they represented Bavaria's superiority to the rest of the republic. "We work for the others," was his standard comment on federalism.

We drove out of the city in the late afternoon. Not far from Riga the dark clouds broke up. A strong wind was driving them northwards. We were heading in the opposite direction, at one hundred and eighty kilometers per hour down narrow, poorly re-surfaced roads. When we came through villages Peter slowed down to a hundred. The villages appeared deserted. Their emptiness contrasted with nature, which was in full bloom. This disproportion lent nature an artificial beauty. The trees, meadows, woods were like paintings. Our destination was Warsaw. We intended to arrive there in the night and then catch the first flight for Munich at six in the morning. For Peter that meant being in his office by nine. Evidently the thought of this punctuality reassured him and enabled him to mobilise his last reserves of strength.

Peter had been watching me as I chatted to the Americans and had judged me to be a skilled negotiating partner. He could use someone like me in his company. This was typical of him. One never knew exactly what was in his mind when he was watching.

Talking to him I defended the advantages of my unattached life. I would simply have stayed an extra day in Riga, enjoying the beauties of the city. Peter vehemently disagreed. The pressure of deadlines and a proper appointments diary were necessary in order to get things done, he said. To underline this, he added: "If you had the necessary discipline you'd have long since written a decent novel. Instead you keep writing all these long-winded short pieces. A novel is a building which has to be built tenaciously and systematically. One can't be working on the roof when the foundations are not yet in place."

That evening I didn't feel like arguing with him over his building site theory. By now it was dark and I was tired.

Suddenly I felt pleased by the thought that I would never finish writing my first novel.

I shut my eyes.

I had no intention of getting involved in Peter's business. It would have meant the end of our friendship. Not because we wouldn't have worked well as business partners. Rather, our relationship would have acquired a different character. For Peter, I represented the dark half of his heart, where his artistic arteries ran. I would not have been immune to power and fame. Peter sometimes tended towards a calm casualness extraordinary in one in his position. To maintain the balance in our relationship, neither one of us could abandon his standpoint. At most we might have swapped roles, but we both lacked any desire to do that.

Close relationships between men have become more feminine. Friendships used to be focused on an external object. It might be a football, some sort of weapon, or a job. Friends had common goals. Nowadays it can happen that men develop intimacies with one another. Standing as if naked facing one another, one allows oneself to be touched, lets one's organism be opened up and explored, makes shared experiences central. Feelings are getting more important. Deeds are receding into the background.

I decided in favour of Berlin and Marie. For the first time in my life I wanted to face up to a challenge. I wanted to come to grips with my origins. That meant not avoiding Marie's sceptical questions, not averting my gaze from the past. Remembering is painful. Memory is the only wound in a person that never fully closes. Not that it is fatal. On the contrary, the pains it causes give life sharper contours.

I had no identity. People around me had increasing problems with this. It was as if the fall of the Wall, the collapse of the old order, had not only had a liberating effect. Without the Wall one felt suddenly unprotected. Identity has become a surrogate concept for feeling protected. One gets a fix on oneself, the other, his origin, in order to determine proximities and distances. It was possible to run into invisible walls anywhere, erected since the fall of the Wall. The world had become more complicated, the paths more labyrinthine. Before, one could have abandoned oneself to playfulness without worrying, felt comfortable losing one's way, the Wall afforded protection from the abyss. Nowadays everyone watched their every step, the very next encounter might trip them up. So my path would lead me inexorably into the past. I could not avoid bringing it into the present.

Suddenly I was no longer a stranger in Berlin. I was not just at home here. I belonged here too. I was one of many moles in the city. We ensured that the ground on which the new capital was to be built always remained loose and treacherously unstable. We loved the sand of Brandenburg.

11

One of the first things I acquired on my return to Berlin was a television set. By now Berlin had cable television, a choice of 28 channels in all. This might not compare with the range in America, but still it was a fair number. When I was in the flat I usually had the television on like a radio. Sometimes I even forgot to turn it off when I went out. For Marie this was unbearable, a deplorable form of behaviour which she ascribed to my Turkish genes. The only reason why the argument about the television did not have catastrophic consequences for our relationship was that Marie spent most of her time out of the flat and I did not insist on having it on in her presence. Having the television on is not the same as watching television. In my opinion, having the television on is the appropriate use of the medium, whereas the practice of sitting down in front of it with a glass of beer and a bowl of crisps is bound to lead in time to the death of important brain cells. I for one do not worship the television, I have it on, sometimes listening, only looking when something interests me, occasionally switching channels. Usually a news channel is on, or MTV, or one of the many local stations which even permit the use of bad German. When I'm missing America, I have CNN on all day, despite the fact that this channel seems to cover the whole world and is hardly suited to quell my longing for the prairie. There are also Turkish, Greek, Kurdish, Persian, Alevite and various religious programmes. The zealots' programmes tend to have poor picture quality. One has to turn the volume down. Since I can't understand Turkish I pay attention to the gestures, the clothing, the way men and women interact, in order to guess who might have made the programme. Without these stations, Berlin would not be a metropolis. Even if they only address their own tribe, with no universal ambitions. Tribal television has a future in the multimedia age. Which is the public or private station that offers the chance to experience a preacher in front of a tapestry decorated with leaping flames, gesticulating wildly as he delivers what is clearly a sermon of warning, frequently repeating the word Sodom. State borders are simply shifted here. A young man sits in front of a map of the near east, in the middle of which an enormous area is outlined in red, its borders running through four countries. Anything is possible. But on what scale? Does everyone who has a globe on their desk have experience of the world? The works of mystics tell us that only he who overcomes the world experiences it. Is it possible to overcome the world in aeroplanes? Human kind is bound up with the world as never before. We have dared too low and too high, we have travelled too far from our centre, and those who seek it, the seekers, are lost. They hasten much too fast towards one another, following old maps which do not show the new paths. They see and yet recognize nothing.

12

By adopting a stricter daily routine I tried to bring order into my life. Time never meant much to me. I did not count and order the moments in my life. Rather I was part of a stream which had set me in the world and which I could do little to resist. But now, for the first time in my life, I was trying to sight land, to find something to hold onto. Of course I knew that the stream that carries one along cannot be stopped, but at least I wanted to set the pace myself.

I regularly visited the city archives. My reading concentrated on the thirties. I read the newspapers of the period, trying to form a comprehensive picture of opinions and moods. History always has a used-up side and an un-used-up side. On the used-up side the historians labour. They attempt to reconstruct. I wanted to work on the un-used-up side. I knotted together the threads in my mind to form the idea of a novel with my grandfather as its central figure. My task was to construct what could not be reconstructed. Grandfather might have been a character invented just for this purpose. Much in his life had remained concealed. His death was mysterious, ultimately unsolved. I had his diaries which I could not read. What did I need the archives for? What were they but an impersonal memory? There was nothing for me to remember. I had to extract my material from that secret place which had supplied my literary production so far. Yet I sensed it was different this time. Where was the my grandfather located? I had guidelines. I had a concrete character before my eyes. And I had Marie as my partner and competitor, working on her subject-matter with meticulous precision. She worked with iron discipline. She did not begin the creative work until she had assembled all the necessary materials. Whereas I had to collect whilst being creatively at work. I intended to use the collected material to pose critical questions about my creations, if necessary to correct them. Marie did not believe in this method. She believed in the existence of various chambers in the brain which cannot be opened simultaneously. "One is for collecting and storing, the other for processing. It's like in the human body, things mustn't get mixed up." Marie loved biological similes. She had studied biology for several semesters before deciding on German and history. Her real passion though was film, documentary film to be precise. Feature films were in her view merely an insignificant variation of the medium. "You should have lived in the twenties," I said, trying to provoke her, "in revolutionary Russia, you'd have been Stalin's first woman of film." Indeed, Marie's library included several works by Russian film theorists, especially those who held that film, documentary film of course, was the only form of representation that was realistic and therefore appropriate to the revolution. What was really the case? How can one represent reality without appearing in it oneself? Later, what was at stake was not a crude realism but a mystic realism. This was also far better suited to the Russian soul. The only reality that had to be shown was ideology. But Marie admired neither Stalin nor the Russian documentarists. Her idol was Leni Riefenstahl. She particularly loved her Olympic films. A large picture showing the artist in one of her Alpine films hung in our hallway over the chest of drawers with the telephone on it. Marie's aberration amused me. Such a perfect person had to have a flaw that made her human. A fanatical supporter of the Green-Alternative ticket – she always called the Greens the 'Alternatives' –, she admired Leni Riefenstahl, the woman who had put her art in the service of Hitler. But great numbers of German artists had done so at that time, was her defence. Those who went into exile were Jewish artists above all, and in many cases not necessarily because they were against Hitler, but because Hitler was against them. They were in exile not primarily because they opposed the regime, but purely and simply because they had lost their right to existence in their own country.

I was always fascinated by the life of exiles. I made great efforts not to idealise it. I read a lot of autobiographies in order to gain a lively sense of the period and people's feelings. Well written autobiographies bring the author back to life. They create a personal relationship between the author and the reader.

Perhaps in this I was also thinking of my mother's family. They had been quiet exiles. My grandad, a successful merchant from liberal German-Jewish circles, despised Hitler so much that all his life he refused to take any interest in the "corporal", as he called him dismissively. My grandad claimed that a branch of our family had set out for Turkey from Regensburg in the sixteenth century. There were records of their departure, but none of their arrival and further existence in Turkey. Probably they had perished on the way from hostilities and disease. In 1916, as a cadet, my grandad had been in Constantinople, as he called Istanbul, to the irritation of my father. He was in the division commanded by Liman von Sanders, but had not seen action in the Dardanelles. There the Turks, under German command, had inflicted a serious defeat on the Allies. "I was in the same division as Mustafa Kemal Pasha," he related proudly. My grandad never called him Ataturk. The time in Turkey must have stayed in his memory. When Hitler came to power he was one of the first to pack his bags. He had no illusions about the future. In early 1934 the family moved to Istanbul, into an old konak on the hills of Çamlıca. My granny had wanted to live amid green, as in Munich-Grünewald. From the garden there was a fascinating view of the huge yet idyllic city with the fairy-tale minarets on the horizon. Grandad found a good job with a firm of insurance brokers.

The German exile community in Istanbul grew fast. Many scholars came to the city. In Ankara there was rejoicing. The government wanted to modernize backward Turkey as quickly as possible. Turkey was to become a European state, severed from its oriental traditions. The Germans were the answer to a prayer. It was almost incomprehensible that Hitler could drive the most capable scientists out of his country. An agency in Switzerland arranged postings for lawyers, economists, architects and philologists at Turkish universities, in faculties founded especially for them. The

German scientists and scholars not only brought with them the spirit of the Enlightenment, they even rolled up their sleeves in all humility to carry books into the libraries. Coming from universities with rich traditions, they became pioneers. These men shaped the image of Germany in Turkey to far more lasting effect than Hitler with his big speeches and his eccentric personality. In the First World War it had been the talent for organisation and the personal bearing of the German officers, now it was the unaffected manner and the creative qualities of the scientists and artists that won the hearts of many Turks. Hardly any voices portrayed them as traitors to their country or made anything of their mostly Jewish origins. Most of the Germans quickly learned Turkish, like my grandparents, and soon they hardly felt they were in exile, rather in a second homeland. It was easy to make contact with Turks, even if it might take longer for relations to grow more intimate.

When war broke out, the atmosphere in Istanbul too grew harsher. Food was rationed.

One of the best hotels in the city was the "Tokatlıyan", Grandad's favourite hotel. He regularly enjoyed a couple of drinks there after work. The hotel belonged to an Armenian family. As Hitler's rapid successes at the front led to his popularity rising, the hotel became a meeting point for the old-established German community in Istanbul which was dominated by Nazis, and plotted against the exiles. The hotel flew the National Socialist flag. Istanbul's Jewish community called for a boycott of the hotel.

The Christian minorities in Turkey cultivated a centuries-old hatred of Jews. The majority of Turkish Jews had come as refugees from Spain. They had always been loyal subjects of the Sultans. But the Christians saw them as allies of Islam in its struggle against Christianity in Europe. These feelings were strengthened by the growth of nationalism. Jews and Turks became interchangeable hate figures for Christian Greeks and Armenians.

As the World War progressed the pressure on Turkey from Hitler's

Germany grew. The exiles found themselves caught between the front lines ever more often. Among friends, Grandad would often tell of this period. One anecdote I remember precisely.

There were two German booksellers in the city, Mühlbaur and Kalis. The exiles met in one, the Nazi supporters frequented the other. Here one could buy the official Nazi daily, "Völkischer Beobachter". This proved the bookseller's downfall. In August 1940 the "Völkischer Beobachter" published an anti-Turkish cartoon. The bookseller Kalis was arrested for disseminating this cartoon. In order to snub racist Germany, when he was arrested he was handcuffed to a black policeman.

My grandad was one of those German Jews to whom Judaism meant nothing more than the faith of their fathers. The maternal side of my family had been committed to the Enlightenment for generations. In my grandad's view the humanism of the German Enlightenment tradition was the only valid religion of his time. It would never have occurred to him to convert to Christianity, for he regarded this religion as no less outdated than Judaism. In fact my grandparents had always put up a Christmas tree, and as I learned from my mother, they continued to do so in Turkey. My mother must also have prevailed over my father as regards the Christmas tree, for it is a fixture of my childhood. For me, from way back, religion was the most important incidental fact in the world.

The world religions occupy much of my thought. But for me they were always other people's faiths. Had I wanted to have a faith, I would never have been able to choose among the many different variants of proof of God's existence. So I became a non-believer who is interested in religions in the same way that a globetrotting backpacker is interested in foreign countries. I would often read big books about the history of religion. They were as exciting as murder stories. My interest in general history came later.

My grandparents had returned to Munich a few years after the war. The house the Nazis had seized had been restored to them, and my grandad worked as a buyer for a Munich company. My parents only followed in 1954, the year of my birth. My mother wanted me to be born in Germany. She set great store by me becoming a German. Thus after my birth, Turkish was no longer spoken at home, though surely it must have been earlier now and then. When I grilled her with my questions, she explained these decisions in terms of wishing to spare me an uncomfortable life between two stools. In view of my subsequent career, she must later have considered her project a failure.

I began asking questions at the age of seven. Perhaps even earlier, but that is as far back as I can remember. When I was ten my grandad died, his wife a year later, a very elegant but otherwise rather inconspicuous woman. All I remember is that she would lie down in the late afternoon every day and only get up after sunset. She called this odd habit "going to bed with the day".

Since my father was seldom there and my mother remained taciturn, at some point I stopped asking questions about my grandad and shut myself into his large library on the ground floor. My grandad had built it up in the twenties. It was full of first editions from the period, German but also many French and some American books. As if by a miracle, most of the books had survived the vandalism of the Nazi period in wine cases in the cellar, where grandad had packed them personally before he fled. A list of the authors quickly made clear that many were those whose works had been burned by the Nazis. Besides literature, this massive library mostly consisted of historical and philosophical works. Thomas Mann quickly became my favourite writer. I admired the creative discipline emanating from his work. But I also read a great deal at random, unable to put a book down even if I understood nothing and had already begun reading another one. Each time I finished a book I wrote down my thoughts and above all my questions in a large notebook. I set myself the task of answering these questions bit by bit, though I could never find complete answers. Ever since, I have been sceptical about any kind of understanding. I believe that in many matters we are far too quick to signal that we understand, whether because of the power instinct, or out of fear. My way of asking questions developed out of this sceptical attitude. For other people my endless questions were a source of irritation, especially as I often continued asking questions when things seemed to have been settled. I was told that in this I was like my grandad. It was no accident that I felt like his representative in the library, charged with the duty of reading everything through once again.

There were no survivors in my mother's family. This was never mentioned. My mother's response to my questions, which mostly followed the discovery of photos in one of the library's many drawers, was annoyance. She took the photos off me and, as I later discovered, described aunts and cousins as strangers and friends of Grandad. "You wouldn't have understood back then," she said later when I tackled her about this. "Even we grown-ups were unable to understand what had happened." I have never lost the feeling that they were hiding the German catastrophe from me so that I would be able to establish an unbroken relationship to this country. Perhaps she was ashamed of these deeds which had been done in her country, even though her family belonged to the victims and not to the perpetrators. I often observed this phenomenon among victims of the Hitler regime. Their hatred for the regime never led them to hate Germany or to damn the Germans as a people. One behaves almost as if someone in one's own family had done something wrong. One is shocked and ashamed and wants to get over the incident as quickly as possible. Such people were always very lonely with their grief. In contrast to this, Jews who had only come to Germany after the catastrophe behaved very differently. Some of them turned their Jewish identity into a profession. They spoke out. The conscience of the Germans must be appealed to and must remain burdened for ever. They travelled from one site of remembrance to the next, made speeches, gathered people around them. Memory was the lingua franca that united them all. But these people too remained lonely.

They were often the only survivors in their family. Some reproached themselves for having survived. They were strangers wherever they went.

13

Our grief is not governed by our feelings but by the calendar. We have to perform grief. All the mourners know one another from public occasions. They acknowledge one another with nods, and all of them know where they have to stand. There is a gathering around a stone memorial, in a place where the place-name stands in for the names of the victims we are here to remember. We grieve because we lack something. We have had to spend a long time searching in the labyrinth of grief to find out what we lack. We have had to discover that we are mourning for something we lost not long ago. The victims are dead. The perpetrators live. We are no longer able to remember. We are mourning for memory. For the perpetrators there are no surviving victims. All the survivors are perpetrators. This is the basis for the reconciliation between perpetrators and victims. Grief hides from the mourners their reason for mourning. This phenomenon is called feeling deeply affected. Perpetrators and victims mourn in common in the name of feeling deeply affected. Grief, of all conditions of the soul the most corporeal, connecting heart, mind, and bodily fluids together directly, becomes feeling deeply affected when the body of grief vanishes completely in the body of the griever. Feeling deeply affected is the appropriate state to be in on days of remembrance, a sentimental concept negating bodily grief. When grief is not expressed by individuals but performed by a group, feeling deeply affected has taken over from grief. It is the birth of farce from the spirit of tragedy.

14

I have no idea why I always imagined the Nazis in pyjamas. In my imagination they wore those classic striped pyjamas which unfortunately also recall prison uniform. For all that my mother left the Nazi years unmentioned, they became important to me. As early as my schooldays I had secretly begun collecting photos from that time. I had a series with buildings, large buildings with pale facades, and another series with men in uniform. I imagined that men like these must have built these buildings, and I was unable to comprehend how a generation so obsessed with building could have launched a war which put all they had created at risk. The random collection of photos led to a passion for collecting. I began collecting newspapers and magazines from the thirties, everyday objects, and above all manuscripts. In my grandfather's library I had found some books about graphology. Handwriting reveals far more about a person than a photo. A photo is usually taken by another person. It is the gaze of a stranger made permanent. Handwriting is made by one's own hand, it is fully a part of one's self.

I collected manuscripts, brief notes, sometimes on paper, sometimes on beermats or matchboxes, letters, drafts. I arranged the manuscripts according to a strict hierarchy, following the order of ranking within the National Socialist state system. I had nothing by the Führer, but I had a short letter by Goering postponing an appointment, some notes by Speer, letters from local gauleiters and from artists who were close to the regime. For a long time I was unsure where to place the artists in the hierarchy, until I decided to put them on a par with the gauleiters. No doubt this amounted to demotion for some, while for others it was favourable treatment, but it fitted. My passion for collection turned me into an autograph hunter. When a German magazine believed it had discovered Hitler's diaries, I knew from the beginning that it had to be a fake, albeit a very skilful one. A few weeks later all was revealed. Once again history could not be rewritten. The likeable writer of the diaries was not Hitler. All the years I was assembling my collection of manuscripts I was surprised how few people were interested in them. Fewer people still knew about the subject. So again and again I was able to purchase important documents for a song. While the demand for medals and other mostly worthless symbols from the Nazi period rose, fewer and fewer people were interested in the manuscript documents. Perhaps people were projecting onto the past the fact that handwriting was becoming less significant in their own everyday lives.

Berlin also proved to be an ideal place for collecting. There were many private archives with unknown material. For a while I advertised in the "Berliner Zeitung" and in a classified freesheet, and every week at least two, sometimes up to ten people contacted me. They were usually widows clinging to the edge of the abyss. They did not want their documents to go to an archive of the Federal Republic and were visibly delighted that a private person was interested, especially since in my case it was a polite, well informed, correctly dressed young man, whose short blonde hair and blue eyes seemed to qualify him as the ideal recipient of the material on offer. The old ladies were seldom brusque and always offered me at least a cup of coffee. I was surprised how alike the décor of their flats was. Everywhere the same yellow-brown wallpaper, cumbersome antique furniture, heavy Persian carpets that took up almost the whole of the living-room floor. Some ladies gave me a tour of the flat, showing me photos of their children and grandchildren. Money was seldom an issue. They wanted to know that their past was in safe hands, that was all. Several had been enthusiastic members of the League of German Girls and had kept many documents and manuscripts from that period. But most of the ladies were older still, they remembered the First World War and told me stories of the inflation, how all they possessed became worthless from one day to the next and so on. A good many of them still blamed the Jews for this. The inflation and the Hitler years apparently occupied their entire memories. On one occasion a woman living in a very elegant and well kept house in Dahlem told me that the Turks nowadays were far worse than the Jews back then. The Jews had worn the mask of Germanness. They had simply acted as if they were Germans. One hadn't been taken in of course. But then that had been their problem. She thought for a while and then added that Jews and Germans had been united by a love-hate relationship. But between Germans and Turks there was only hatred.

I hardly ever went to auctions. What was on offer was meagre, the prices were inflated, the people simply boring.

When I left Berlin for America my manuscript collection amounted to exactly 520 items. I decided against taking it with me. I left the manuscripts, the photos, with the insects and various other things I had collected, carefully packed up in my mother's house in Munich.

I will not let the house. There should be a place in my life where my past is preserved and remains accessible to me.

15

I came back from America with a different relationship to the new media. In fact it was there that I first established any kind of relationship to computers as a means of communication. Networks enabled the isolated prairie to move into the centre of world events. Back in Berlin I soon noticed that this European metropolis lay far from the highways of worldwide information exchange. No one in my circle of acquaintance was making use of the opportunity to send electronic mail. The Internet was a laboratory experiment. When after careful consideration I decided to learn Turkish, I had a surprise. Several young men and women who had taken a course with me at the Technical University proved to be not just Turks who no longer knew their mother tongue – or in my case, father tongue – but also open to new technologies and members of a computer club. This club purported to be an association for people who spent their free time getting up to date with the latest computing technology. In fact the association had rented rooms in a former hat factory in a northern part of the city, which now offered space to various alternative projects. At almost any time, one found these rooms occupied by young people wearing baseball caps back to front, sitting at computers. Soon I had made friends with them and invited them to a literary event at which once again, after a long break, I read from new work. Apart from Marie they were the only people in the audience. I read some poems and afterwards we went to my local in Kreuzberg. In the course of this evening, which they later assured me they had enjoyed, they came to confide in me, and soon I was privy to the club's secrets. The group was working on new software which would not only enable information to be transmitted, but would also alter the information in transit. The aim was to make it possible to encode certain secret data in such a way as to make it absolutely impossible for unauthorised persons to obtain access to it. But the possibility would also be created of influencing and disrupting information pathways. They made their work out to be somehow illegal, though I could see nothing illegal about it. I assured them that I would tell no one. If I am writing this now, it is only because by now one can purchase the programme in any software store, naturally only as a means of protecting files. The association has developed into a well established company with joint ventures in the USA, Japan and Kazakhstan. Meanwhile the members of the group speak fluent Turkish and are in the process of setting up a branch in Istanbul. I myself dropped out of the Turkish course a few weeks later. I felt that this new language would not bring me further at the moment. With the help of the Arabic alphabet I was already able to make out some words in grandfather's diaries. But this vocabulary brought him no closer to me. In the end, unknown words separated me from his life.

A man with such clear handwriting cannot have anything to hide, I said to myself.

16

Architects have to shape not only space but also time. They are great changers of times. When a city's centre is completely rebuilt, new times dawn. People always resist a change of times. It makes them feel as if the ground is being pulled from under their feet. A change of times either means a rebirth or a feeling that one's own time has run out. The society is deeply split.

"Berlin faces a test of its worth." With this phrase, measures were introduced in the city which were believed to be important. The phrase was meant to function like a heading in an invisible text, designed to attract the attention of the reader or listener. The success of such headings will be familiar to everyone from their schooldays: one woke up, felt hungry, and thought about break and a snack.

I end conversations which begin with this kind of phrase by excusing myself, saying I have to go home to take a phone call, or if by mischance the conversation is taking place in my own home, I glance repeatedly at the clock and fidget nervously. If this still does not help, I stand up and walk around the room once or twice. People have generally disappeared from the flat within half an hour of this. There are stubborn cases of course, where the only solution is to fall asleep with one's eyes open.

Berlin is a young city, not a city where one dwells for long on ancient history. This city's challenge is the future. People here have always lived looking ahead. So the Wall will soon be forgotten. One feels one is part of a gigantic experiment. No one can predict what the city will look like in ten years or twenty. Everyone in the city is an architect in his own way.

Berlin is bidding to host the Olympic Games in 2000. Is it possible to shape the future with no memory? Or can there only be a better future on the basis of memory? The bid is half-hearted. Opponents of the Olympics have been undermining its chances from the outset. The city where in this century two ideologies collapsed has become level-headed. The rubble is to be cleared away, the waste land to become the construction site for a functional life-world. But can lies that lives are lived by be cleared away like building debris? The decay of ideologies has left behind worn-out bodies, their powers of resistance broken, their imaginations and their living spirits flown. Too out of practice for games, not sporty enough.

17

Marie has gone to Thessaloniki on the trail of Talat Pasha. He worked as a teacher in a Jewish grammar school there. At the same time he was the underground leader of the Party of Unity and Progress, which was fighting against the Sultan for an Ottoman Empire of free citizens. Talat Pasha was responsible for the deportation of hundreds of thousands of Armenians in the Ottoman Empire during the First World War. How could a successful, enlightened politician have become a mass murderer? Was the key to the answer in Thessaloniki?

In the decaying Ottoman Empire, Thessaloniki had been the centre of modernization. A cosmopolitan port inhabited by Christians, Jews, and Moslems, where one spoke French, drank German beer, and could get rich in trade. What will Marie find there now? Surely not anyone who knew Talat. They would have to be over a hundred years old to remember him now. Thessaloniki is not a city where people live to be a hundred. I spent twenty-four hours there once. That was enough. The sea stinks over the city. With its damp, warm, mouldy breath. The houses are faded, not even gleaming in the sunshine. Thessaloniki is the refugees' city. In 1912 Jews and Turks leave the city. The city becomes Greek. Jews who remain under Greek rule survive, barely, until Hitler comes. Marie was surprised to discover in the course of her research that most of the Jews had left the city along with the Turks. She had never heard about Greek anti-Semitism. In Germany only the German form of anti-Semitism is known. As if it stopped at the German borders. As if it were not also to be found in Poland and Russia, among Greeks and Armenians, Bulgarians and Romanians. The collapse of the Ottoman Empire was no less of a catastrophe for the Jews of the Balkans than it was for the Turks. No power now protected them from persecution. The Christians were not merely potentially anti-Semitic, they remembered very clearly the closeness and harmony between Jews and Turks in the Ottoman Empire.

The Jews had arrived in the Ottoman Empire long before as refugees from Spain and had always remained gratefully attached to the Empire. They put their skills in the service of the Sultans. They were good technicians and doctors. The Ottoman army and the health of the Pashas and Sultans profited from this. The French ambassador to the Sublime Porte reported home in 1551:

"Especially remarkable is the immense number of Jews residing in Turkey and Greece, but notably in Constantinople. Still their numbers continue to rise, which is due to the fact that almost everywhere in the Empire they are engaged in trade in goods and money, the most various kinds of goods from all countries of the world being brought here by sea and by land. It is beyond doubt that the trade and finance of the entire Levant is nowadays largely in Jewish hands. It is they who are the owners of the very greatest entrepots and shops stocked with the most various goods. Also not seldom to be found among them are skilled craftsmasters and manufacturers, notably among the Marranos recently driven out of (fled from) Spain and Portugal. To the great injury of Christendom these people are teaching the Turks about various discoveries in war equipment, such as the fabrication of artillery shot, arquebuses, powders, munitions and so forth. Similarly it is the Jews here who are establishing printing workshops, hitherto unknown in Turkey, where they are printing Latin, Greek, Italian, Spanish and Hebrew books; only they are not permitted to make Turkish and Arabic books on their printing presses. Further, Jews display great knowledge of languages, so that they are much in use as interpreters."

I will not travel in pursuit of my characters. Talat Pasha is no concern of mine. He is Marie's project. He will not lead me to grandfather, I cannot find him anywhere. My parents left their country long ago. No things are being kept there for me still which have any instantly obvious value for the present. Architects of forgetting build their pompous structures into the draughty gaps in memory. When I look into this country's history, I see nothing.

18

I have begun collecting old maps. The territories vary in size but always appear empty, where all these meaningless borders, drawn with much blood, are preserved.

On a map from the year 1869 the borders of the Ottoman Empire stretch far into Europe. It is two hundred years since the Turks were beaten back outside Vienna. They still have European subjects. The "Turkish yoke" is still a set phrase, although the "Turkish threat" seems to have been dispelled. Fear of the Turks is disguised at masquerades as fascination with the Turks.

A map from 1913. New states have come into existence in the Balkans. The borders of the Ottoman Empire recall the borders of contemporary Turkey.

Turks and Greeks, Armenians, Jews and Kurds, Circassians, Albanians, Bosnians, Bulgarians, Assyrians and Georgians. They had lived together for eight hundred years, not always in peace, but they had survived living together. Even the Turks were not just Turks, they were Sunnis or Alevis, and the Alevis were peasants or craftsmen in the city, nomads or hunters, holy and unholy, heretical and pious. They were not just dark-haired with corn-coloured skin, they were also blonde with turquoise-blue eyes, "blue" and "sky" were the same word in their language.

Then foreign teachers came – here foreigner was the word for anyone who had travelled far – and gave them names: Turkish ones for the Turks, Kurdish ones for the Kurds, Alevite ones for the Alevis. No one was to go by another's name. The families were split, the children grew up as foreigners. Turks became Greeks because they were Christians, Greeks became Turks because they were Moslems. They saw one another as foreign. Foreigner was the word for a neighbour who had never travelled.

19

Tell the story, tell the story, just as it happened. Tell it even if it's not your own story. At some point you heard it and forgot it again, then you remembered it again and couldn't believe it. One doesn't have to believe every story one hears. There would be no stories at all if all of them were real. The contours of reality are sharpest at the borders of dreaming. Truth and imagination are in dispute. Your grandfather was a powerful man. He died a powerless death which no one mentions. No one has understood why he ended his life prematurely. Was he so obsessed with power that he even wanted to gain power over death? Did he have an incurable sickness? Was business going badly? A rich, influential man ends his life as it reaches its peak. Grandfather had spent his life on borders drawn with blood. A trauma from the war must have stayed with him. Cruelty can give a person power, strengthen them, but can also split them apart if they cannot resist the inner pressure from their conscience. Contradictory feelings, pleasure and pangs of conscience split their consciousness. How can I heal a dead man's wounds if I don't know what he died of?

Grandfather was a member of the Olympic team. He was seen as the wrestlers' patron. He was supposed to accompany the team to Berlin. He knew a smattering of German.

Between 1933 and 1935 the volume of German-Turkish trade grows by almost 150%. The statistics reveal a considerable increase in the Turkish population in the Berlin of the thirties. In 1933, 585 Turks are living in the capital of the Reich. By 1938, 3300.

The white shirts must be spotless. The Turkish team is practising marching and giving the German salute for their entrance into the Olympic stadium in Berlin. The German Führer will be present. Everyone agrees on the advantage of the German salute: it disciplines. The lifted arm brings the body into an erect posture. A masculine gesture, quite different from the effeminate wave.

20

I usually begin my texts when half asleep. Language and dream are in competition then. I always have pen and paper by the bed. I can get no rest until I've noted everything down. Words I don't write down get lost again. Retrieving them is harder than fetching a lost ring from a deep well. Sleep is for the poet what the sea is for fishermen. Hunting ground, home, foreign country.

21

I can't stop. I'm visiting the State Library regularly again. Before I went away to America I was there every day. Each morning I was one of the first to get there. I usually went to the Oriental section, but did not always sit at the same table, as most others did. I felt it suited my situation in life better if I changed tables. The Oriental section was not yet crowded then. One could easily find a table.

Now everything had completely changed. If one did not come early every table was occupied and one had to find a corner to sit on the floor in the broad corridors of this great tent for readers. So I got used to getting up early again. It only took a few days to rediscover old friends. Most were now finishing the work they were writing.

Mehmed was writing a dissertation on Mehmed the Second, the conqueror of Constantinople. He was investigating the Ottoman Sultan's concept of the state. In his view, the Sultan had been a socialist at the bottom of his heart.

Susanne was from Bremen and was writing a dissertation in the law faculty on torture techniques in the middle ages. She had devoted one chapter to impaling. She had given me this chapter to read with the comment that impaling had been invented by the Orientals. In twenty-eight pages she gave a short history of this method of punishment, followed by an exact description of the various techniques for enabling the victim to survive being impaled for as long as possible. I gave the work back to her with the comment that all this impaling very much put me in mind of sexual intercourse. Did she know of any study of the sexual connotations of the practice? I mentioned the books of Bataille in order to make clear how seriously I meant this observation. But Susanne took back the manuscript without a word and left me standing. Since then she does not acknowledge me.

Heinrich was a historian writing a history of circumcision in Germany. I well remember the scene in the cafeteria when we had our first encounter. I was waiting in the queue to get a cup of coffee. Heinrich was standing just behind me. I had noticed him before, for his head was unusually large for his body. His reddish blonde hair was usually long and unkempt. He had long sideburns covering half his cheeks. His face was full of freckles. Big blue eyes suggested openness and approachability. The long sharp nose was somehow rascally. Heinrich tapped me on the back. I turned round. "Are you circumcised, by any chance?" I was consternated for a moment. But then the question amused me. I put out my hand. "Hi, my name's Sascha." My hand was still in the air when Heinrich nudged me forwards. "You're next." We drank our coffees together. Later, this afternoon coffee became a fixed ritual. We never met outside the library, never went anywhere together, knew little about each other's private lives. Heinrich's girlfriend was a young Turk. He was proud to have snatched her from the clutches of her despotic father. Sometimes it is stimulating not to have much personal information about a conversation partner, especially when one has issues in common. Heinrich and I had a few.

"The body is the only country that a person has," Heinrich stated categorically.

I contradicted him. "Language is far more important. Only in language can one make oneself at home."

"Language alienates people from themselves," he argued. "Man is a nameless being."

Heinrich was an expert on German-Jewish history in the nineteenth century. Since the books I was reading were almost all from this inexhaustible century, his tips were always important for me. Heinrich had read everything written in Germany in the nineteenth and twentieth centuries about circumcision.

"The Germans have learned nothing from history," he remarked casually once. "Now they've brought the Turks into the country. And they couldn't even cope with the Jews."

From the windows of the State Library one has a wide view over the scarcely built-up centre of Berlin. Here the city gives the impression that it has abandoned itself and is hanging as a gigantic dark cloud in the sky above its own territory. Will the cloud now settle back down in the city? Or will it disperse? In Berlin it is not very likely that a cloud will disperse without leaving evident traces. So one must be prepared for quite a lot to happen. Which Berlin is hiding in there? The Prussian Berlin, the cosmopolitan Berlin, the fascist, the socialist, the capitalist, the alternative Berlin, the no-man's-land?

22

In 1910 the anthropologist Franz Boas, the founder of modern American anthropology, accepts a commission from the US congress. He is to write a report describing the development of the American immigrant races. Boas concludes that the bodies of the second generation of immigrant Jews, Sicilians, and Neapolitans differ from the bodies of the first generation. Immigrants' children born in the USA have bigger bodies, lighter skin and a larger brain capacity. They come closer to the European type. Their integration seems more easily possible.

The other culture only exists in the other body. Many immigrants give their children a lot of milk to drink. Milk, they believe, makes the skin lighter and ensures a strong body and healthy teeth. A healthy body cannot have bad teeth.

I note down sentences for re-use later in the appropriate place. I always have two notebooks with me when I read. In one of them, I have given it the title "Inventions", I write down my thoughts and ideas. Sometimes I manage sentences like: "Between the inexpressible and the banal lies the everyday". The other notebook, which I have called "Memories", is for quotations from the books I read. This notebook tends to fill up fast, so that I already have several "Memories", whereas there is only one half-full "Invention". It can sometimes happen that I mix up the two notebooks, smuggling memories in among inventions or vice versa. I'm not terribly particular about it. I'm not an academic. Not that I am an enemy of academia. But I don't trust academics' findings. Above all I do not believe there can be any objective voice which collects and disseminates knowledge. Our perception of the world is subjective. Warmth, size, strength – these are all relative concepts. Everything measurable remains interchangeable.

23

The Pan-European Association awards its Prince Eugene of Savoy Prize to the German journalist Karl Schumann for his essay The Turkish Threat in Europe.

Karl Schumann is a liberal who is concerned about Europe's future. He believes national health is essential. The quotient of Turks, in his view, is too high, and this is weakening the immune systems of European nations. The reforms of Ataturk enabled the Turks to assume a European guise. But their mask cannot hide the Asian-Oriental features of their character.

The Turks are a master race. They always seek to seize command. The robe of victimhood worn by the Jews does not become the Turks. Unlike the Jews, they will raise the question of power. They will not waste time with the arts and the sciences. Those are not their strengths. They aim to go into the army and politics. For that is what they are best at: making speeches and riding into battle. Good night, Europe!

24

Auntie Hell had thrown Good Girl Eve down into the shaft. Good Girl Eve had only wanted to bring a bowl of milk to Auntie Hell, who had long since lost all her teeth. It was a clear cloudless night with not a star to be seen in the sky. Auntie Hell was lying on her bed. The bed was the only thing that fitted into her cottage. Under the bed the paths branched out. No life was long enough to go down them all. This was where Auntie Hell got the food that made her immortal. Now and again she opened the trapdoor and threw someone down into the shaft like a piece of firewood, in order to keep it warm. They had all thought Auntie Hell was dead and had sent Good Girl Eve to her to tidy up, clear out the wicked thoughts still lurking in the room, and pray for the dead woman's soul. But Good Girl Eve, because she was Good Girl Eve, always knew a little more than the others. Because she was Good Girl Eve, though, she did what the others, who knew less than she did, asked her to do. That was her misfortune. So Good Girl Eve, knowing that Auntie Hell is immortal, went to her, taking a bowl of milk in order to placate her. Auntie Hell had no teeth left but she had a very good memory. A memory is first and foremost a very big hole that the most terrible nightmares rise out of, just when they are not needed. The nightmares draw the dreamers deeper into sleep, in order to trap them in an intolerable situation and pitch them out of sleep. Auntie Hell was at home in this hole. She opened the door for Good Girl Eve, took the bowl from her hands and drank the milk she had brought her. The door was still open and she began to get cold. "I must warm the house up," she said to Good Girl Eve. She pushed the bed aside, opened the trapdoor, picked Eve up by the scruff of the neck like a cat and threw her down into the shaft. Good Girl Eve made not a sound. She had been used to obeying all her life. It got warm again. Good Girl Eve was good, and Auntie Hell was an Auntie.

25

Several generations of German Jews have confronted the question of when and how the Jew can shed his Jewishness in order to be a fully qualified German. Lightening of skin and hair colour, Germanization of language and faith had not freed the Jews from the Jewish disease which they had brought with them out of Egypt. The Jews had had to take upon themselves this tormenting question, which German society put to them, in order to belong. They had refined the question and passed it back. And been given it back again. And so on. This reciprocal process continued until the question was reformulated as: "How can Germany become Jew-free?"

In today's Germany, Jews and Germans no longer face one another alone. Instead, a situation has emerged which corresponds to my personal origin and situation. In Germany now, a trialogue is developing among Germans, Jews, and Turks, among Christians, Jews, and Moslems. The undoing of the German-Jewish dichotomy might rescue both parties, Germans and Jews, from their traumatic experiences. But for this to happen they would have to admit the Turks into their sphere. And for their part, the Turks in Germany would have to discover the existence of the Jews not just as part of the German past, in which they cannot share, but as part of the present in which they live. Without the Jews the Turks stand in a dichotomous relation to the Germans. They tread in the footprints of the German Jews of the past.

I only have these fantasies when I am in a good mood. Reality lends no support to such concrete optimistic ideas. My reality is a dark hole, the breadth or narrowness of which I cannot gauge, in which I can hear others breathing but cannot see them. Language serves us only as a means to overlook ourselves. I live in a void which offers me nothing to which to attach the fraying threads which are meant to connect me to the three parts of my self. Three bucking, blocking parts. Two of them are at each other's throats the moment they think they can ignore the third. Triangular relationships are of course the most complicated kind.

But when the question, who is a German and who is not, is asked today, one looks to the Turks. They provide the test cases for the limits of Germanness. Jews trying to come terms with their Germanness discover the Turks in the mirror.

Mirror, mirror, on the wall, who is the most German of us all? Turks and Jews had a relatively quiet common history. The Jews were the Turks' subjects and as such were well loved. They were deportees who had fled to Turkey to save their lives. Could they not have found an honourable death, rather than accept such humiliation? They were seen as cowards. They had long since not been involved in any war. But they made themselves very useful behind the front. They knew how to built the most sophisticated weapons, leaving the use of them to the Turks. This settled the relationship between Turks and Jews for all time. The Jews were ingenious by nature, the Turks practical, good at taking ruthless measures, at executing. When the state of Israel was founded there was astonishment in Turkey that the Jewish state lasted longer than a couple of months. The Jews not only fought their enemies courageously, they even won. But were these victorious warriors really Jews? For a long time, people in Turkey could not believe that the soldiers were Jews from Israel. There were lots of rumours. Some even believed that the Jews had hired Anatolian warriors and built the best weapons for them, as they used to. It had been an army of Turkish mercenaries that had put the Arabs to flight. Every fantasy hides a past which remains unresolved. If there is a Turkish national vocation, it is that of the mercenary.

What kind of picture did the Jews have of the Turks? The Turkish Jews still remained grateful to the Turks, generations later, for having given them refuge centuries before. Many Jews gave up their Jewishness in order to join with the Turks in losing. The great Turkish empire shrank, became poorer and more backward. The

Jews remained true to the Turks, lost their influence, grew poor. Whereas the Jews of Europe increasingly assumed the Christian Europeans' perspective on the Turks. Especially the German Jews.

For my mother, marrying a Turk was by no means a matter of course. My grandfather came from a well-placed bourgeois family. This was fortunate. He had gained a degree in economics in Switzerland, spoke fluent German and French. On returning to Istanbul, he had taken a leading position in the insurance company which also employed my grandad. My parents got to know one another on a company outing to the Black Sea. My father had spotted my mother at once, but he had to prove his worth over a long period. It was more than five years before my mother accepted him. The arrogance and contempt towards the poor and backward Turks, which German Jews had no inhibitions about expressing, was a consequence of their assimilation. To be assimilated can only mean to take on all the perspectives, judgments and prejudices of the assimilating side. Many Orientalists were German Jews. They ascribed to the Orient eternal despotism, fatalism, immutability and otherness. Who would have thought that their grandchildren would become Orientals again, like their ancient forefathers.

Turks and Jews stand in a special relationship in Germany, but does this mean that they share a mutual regard? The Turks, are they not ignorant peasants, the Jews, are they not ugly and untrustworthy? A Turk can only trust a Turk: this is an old law, so deeply internalised that it need not even be spoken.

I have spent a long time trying to find the devil who stops me from writing. I wanted to break his legs. The devil, of course, is in the detail. But in order to make out details, one must have broken the devil's legs. A catch twenty-two. Someone once said that one never runs out of ideas so long as one still has stories to tell. For when one is telling a story one does not think. And when one does not think, ideas occur to one. It is only when one no longer has any stories that one really has nothing left.

I have stories but no details. Without details stories have no voice. In fact one does not have to invent details. It is enough to observe them. What that means is that the details are always already there.

In order to make out the details, I always get up very early. The transition from night to day is a productive phase. One sees things in a new light. Soberly. Bit by bit, more and more things can be correctly guessed. The growing light must be used to gain clarity about details that disappear from view in full daylight. By evening one can hear voices, if one is all ears. These are echoes of the morning's impressions. The details communicate among themselves. The stories begin to talk, sometimes going on until deep into the night. The transition from day to night is brief. It is dark before one knows it. To make out things as they are, one must remember.

26

After a long break I have accepted a commission again from a newspaper. They have asked me to track down the voices of the voiceless and lead them into language. I'm doing portraits of young Turks in Germany, writing texts in which they themselves speak. The monologue is the appropriate form for our times. I visit hangouts, cafés, discos, mosques. Turks and Germans are much more alike than they want to realize. Both suffer to the same extent from megalomania and inferiority complexes. The condition of the so-called German-Turkish friendship is nothing but an expression of the fact that the rest of the world loathes the Turks just as much as the Germans.

I'm no longer doing the work for money. Maybe I just want to prove to myself that I can still write. Waiting for details silenced me. I cannot even read any more because I get tired at the sight of letters. The newspaper people were pleased I showed up again. In that world I have the standing of an expert. For some reason they think they can trust me blindly. I am seen as a sharp-eyed observer with a sure instinct. In the world I have to describe, instincts are everything. It is the world of the migrants, the marginals. Beyond the centre a different logic rules. My task is to translate this logic. For this reason they even call me "the Translator". Translators know neither truth nor lies. A translator is the others' liar. If he sees a truth that does not match the others' truth he has to keep it to himself. Were he to reveal this truth, the others would just complain about the bad translator. Without translators the world would fall apart in many places. They make many seams invisible. Only those who are too close to the seams feel the pain, the itching and burning where the stitching runs.

Ali, estate agent

Address to the Germans

You sick people! You Germans are sick! You live in one of the loveliest countries on earth. You breed the best shepherd dogs. You're reckoned among the richest. The whole world is convinced you're hard workers. You've got scientists who'd not even go for a leak when they're sitting inventing a formula. You build the best cars, at football you're the greatest of all. So why so discontented, my brothers? It's not even that your women are a bad fuck. And you wail and lament, you wallow about on your great bellies like pigs fattened up for the slaughter. Why this boredom, my brothers? Watch out! Because we're coming! We've learned to love you, we know your talents. We'd rather not have to alter our picture of you. That'd cost you far too dearly. We're Germany's new patriots. Whenever anyone pisses on this country, we're there. We, the far-born, with hardly thirty years behind us in this country. We're a fresh breeze, so get moving! Don't worry, we're not about to slaughter you, we never touch sweet-tasting meat. But you'd better toe the line or we'll get what we can for your flesh in a deal with your neighbours. Where we come from it's roll up your sleeves and get down to it. We're still under your command, don't forget. We apply method to everything. We're tomorrow's Germans. You're useless, you're fat and you're frightened, get out of the way, we're coming! You moaning minnies, I reckon another decent war is what you need, a war to send a rocket up your arses. I won't say it a second time. We've already got people right at the top, moneybags and armour-piercers. You need a firm hand once again. We're here to teach you decency, morality, modesty, you tossers. We'll oil the wheels again. There's too much grit in your gearboxes. One, two, one, two. We're coming to squirt our young fresh oil into you. That'll grease you up. We're crude. We're as crude as you are. Fear no more for the future of this country. We love it. You sick people! We're going to cure you.

Kamile, fashion designer

I am the other child

I was a child twice. Once in Turkish, once in German. As a Turkish child I couldn't yet speak German, as a German child I already spoke Turkish. So the Turkish child learned German. But the German child never had to learn Turkish.

When my childhood is mentioned I never know for sure which is meant, the Turkish or the German. When I see a written word like "ruh", I have to hear how it's spoken before I can understand what it means. The Turkish child translates it for the German child as "ruch", "soul", but the German child shakes her head, she knows exactly what it means. It simply means "ruh", 'quiet', as in be quiet, keep quiet, let's have a bit of quiet.

I don't want to take sides. There'd be no point. Let each believe what she wants to, understand what she wants to, tell the stories she wants to. Each in her own language.

The Turkish child became timid. She met many foreigners. She never grew up. She's alive. But the German child had to think and die in order to grow up. So now I'm a child in Turkish and a grown-up in German. I can say anything, write anything, in whichever language, every one of my words has a Turkish childhood. If the German forgets, the Turkish child remembers. If the Turkish child can't understand, the German explains. Does this work out?

"The Germans are foreigners," my father says. "We don't understand them," my mother says. "There's a lot that divides us." They cherish and care for the Turkish child, making sure she will never grow up. She must always remain as they picture her, well-behaved, innocent, shy. They're afraid of the German woman. She's foreign. They took no notice of her as a child. They weren't sure whether she was their own child.

"It's me," I always say when I visit them. As if my appearance might not be enough for them to recognize me. Yes, it's still me. "We haven't lost you, girl, you're back," my mother cries. My father sings. I'd be able to understand everything, I could have the feeling of being back at home. But

I only nod my head briefly like someone indicating that she's in a hurry and can't stop.

I'd like to ask my parents questions about my German childhood. But they can only remember the Turkish child. In their eyes I am only that one child. My German self is not perturbed. It lets the Turkish child be. The Turkish child grew to be seven years old. Then she became immortal. She talks to herself. Sometimes she writes letters to people she used to know. Letters she can't post, because she doesn't know where they've gone.

Halil, schoolteacher, currently unemployed

Hands off the German women

I've got a German-Turkish girlfriend now. German women and Turkish men, it never works out. My mother always said so. But I didn't want to believe her.

The Germans are selfish people. The Turks are as well, but the Germans are even more selfish. That is, with the Germans the women are selfish too. For example when I slept with my German girlfriend I always asked her if she had come. She said that was one reason why she left me. Her orgasms were her own private concern, she said.

I'll admit we Turkish men aren't half as good lovers as the reputation that precedes us. But somehow we all want to live up to our reputation.

Then there's also the issue with the unshaved legs. That was something my mother always found especially revolting. As far as she was concerned, the fact that most German women don't shave their legs proved that they don't wash properly either. I don't know why she made this connection. It doesn't hold true in my experience.

I was lucky enough to receive a humanistic education, in the course of which they naturally tried to teach me that what counts in a relationship is not the hairs on the woman's legs. But it was no use. The leg-shaving issue disturbs me too. How happy I was when I found out that most French and American women, as well, belong to the Turkish Never-Forget-to-Shave-Your-Legs brigade. Turkish women, French women, American women – so many cultivated nations can't all be wrong. But the Germans remain obstinate.

I've stopped missing my German women. Now I have a German-Turkish girlfriend. She's disillusioned me. She combines the bad characteristics of both sides and so she makes me eternally happy.

Zafer, writer

How I fell among the foreigners

I'm a writer. For some I'm a Turkish writer. This Turkish writer writes his works in German. By now he also has a German passport, but at the same time he still has an unpronounceable name, which as a rule he has to spell out as follows: S for Samuel, E for Emil, N for North Pole, O for Otto, C for Caesar, A for Anton, K for Kaufmann. One exotic sounding name becomes seven familiar ones. Familiar, but to whom? Who in Germany is called Samuel? Who is called Emil? Or North Pole? Is Germany the North Pole of my identity?

When the writer is asked about his identity, this being a very popular question, since the person asking it is almost always unsure of his own, he leans back and begins to recite: Samuel-Emil-NorthPole-Otto-Caesar-Anton ...

Otto was the Bavarian king of Greece, Caesar was a Roman emperor, Anton was the name of my best friend for a long time. We shared the same desk at school, until one day Anton claimed that my stuff – meaning my books and pens – was taking up more space than I was actually entitled to. He took a piece of chalk and drew a straight line which from now on divided the desk exactly where he thought the middle was. I sat at my half, he at his. I was amazed how he had succeeded in drawing such a straight line without a ruler. I couldn't even do it with a ruler. But this border destroyed our friendship, since Anton always mounted reprisals for frontier violations by hitting me with the ruler, and all too often I forgot about the existence of the border.

I'm a child of the seventies. I came to Germany in 1970, to be precise, to Bavaria. This wasn't my first time in Germany. But this time it was for longer. I had to go to school here.

1970: the Social Democrat–Liberal coalition under chancellor Willy Brandt had just come to power. But the people governing Bavaria were different. There was a fat-cheeked, bull-necked politician who was able to pack especially many words into a single sentence when it was his turn to speak on television programmes. And sometimes when it was not his turn to speak. His face reminded me of the expressions on the hunting trophies which hung on the walls of certain inns. These trophies always made a strong impression on me as a child. I knew they came from animals which had been stuffed. I wasn't scared of them. There had to be some reason why they were kept and used to decorate the walls.

When one can't understand a country's language, that country is nothing but a picture calendar. One stands looking at pretty pictures, or not so pretty pictures.

It was the first winter after our arrival in Germany. Anton was visiting me. "Where's your Christmas tree?" he asked, standing in our living room. I asked my mother where our Christmas tree was. My mother asked my father where our Christmas tree was. My father asked God above about the Christmas tree. God above despaired.

Sometimes I went shopping with my parents. We took the tram into town. I loved the blue trams which had their own peculiar smell, which gave me headaches. A highlight of these trips was the visit to the butcher. Butchers shops have always fascinated me. Nowhere else can one see so much blood and raw meat. Our butcher was a friendly, elderly man with a calm, gentle face. He had the usual physical proportions of a butcher. Sometimes he wore a small skullcap, slightly smaller than the one my father owned. The visit to the butcher always involved conversations which I didn't understand. The butcher wasn't alone in the shop. An ancient man with a long beard was often sitting on a chair in a corner. The grey beard probably made him older than he was. He spoke to my father about God, and I didn't understand what God was doing in the butcher's shop. My father called the man with the beard a chacham. He was happy to see him there. "We can be sure that the meat is pure," he said.

On the way to the primary school which I was now to attend – I still couldn't speak a word of German and I was frightened of the moment when I would have to stand in silence facing the other children as they asked questions – my father explained something which completely astounded me, but at the same time gave me an inexplicable feeling of relief: "In Germany you don't kiss the headmaster's hand," he said, "you just shake it, like a friend's." This actually rather casual comment, made by the father of a Turkish boy who until now had been bound up in the authoritarian educational structures of his homeland, stuck in the boy's memory. When we got to the school and stood before the headmaster, I followed my father's instructions and merely shook the man's hand, although the fact that he was not only a headmaster but also a man of advanced years with white hair unambiguously called for a hand-kiss.

After the greeting the man disappeared into a side-room to fetch a chair which he offered to me, an eight-year-old kid. There was something wrong about this country. I looked at my father, who signalled that I should accept the offer and sit down.

How does a child perceive foreignness and foreigners? Isn't everybody a foreigner apart from father and mother?

If one has a secure home, the question of where the house is, is unimportant. Our house was in Germany.

"As a Foreigner in Germany" was the title of a book I was given one day as a present. "You should read this, it's just right for you," remarked my friend Joseph, or Sepp as we all called him, handing me the gift. Sepp also wrote poems, so-called Sepp-poems. They were poems describing the everyday life of a certain Sepp.

At first I was pleased about the book's title. Could I be holding in my hands the catechism that would at last explain what foreignness in Germany was? But leafing through it I was disappointed. The foreignness in this book consisted in the fact that all the authors in the book were foreigners from the point of view of German readers. A writing competition had been organised for them with the theme: "As a Foreigner in Germany". The entries had been collected in the book. I was taken aback. I couldn't understand the logic that excluded Germans, who often feel more foreign in their own country than foreigners do, from taking part in such a competition. Very few of the texts in the book were literary texts. As far as I was concerned the book was a bad joke. But it also had paradigmatic significance. *The more one feels at home in Germany, the closer one gets to the Germans, the more foreign one becomes in German eyes. The Germans have a tendency to smash the mirror in which their image appears. Once a foreigner gets so close that he reflects the Germans, he enters a dangerous zone. Perhaps that's why there are no criteria for immigration in Germany. Mirror images are not tolerated.*

By the time I took the school-leaving exam I had written my first poems in German and published them in Munich punk fanzines, among other places, though I wasn't part of that scene. But the tone of my "urban lyrics", part expressionist and part pessimistic, seemed to appeal to the people in this scene, who were mostly of my generation.

Yet soon at readings I was being asked: What did my texts actually have to do with the lives of Turks in Germany? Why wasn't I writing about the experiences of the gastarbeiters? About xenophobia and racism? People also wanted to know what language I dream in. I was unable to answer these questions. I felt attracted to poets like Rimbaud, Celan, Eich, Huchel, and Bachmann. Novels by Kafka and Camus have always meant more to me than the works of Yaşar Kemal. But there were Turkish writers who fascinated me too: the Istanbul story-teller Sait Faik, whose fragmentary work seemed to me to be the most exemplary attempt to describe the decaying cosmopolitan world of Istanbul.

I've always felt close to this half hidden, half vanished world. I was glad to be able to read poets like Yunus Emre and Behçet Necatigil in the original language. And, later, to be able to translate poems by them into German. These translations enabled me to feel I was getting very close to them. Yet working on these translations was not a homecoming. Turkish in Germany never felt like an island to which I could choose to withdraw. The Turkish in me was just one more window in the house I had built in Germany and in German, a window looking out on a part of my childhood where roots of different flavours run.

In 1992 there was a change of government in Germany. The new chancellor of the new Christian Democrat–Liberal coalition announced a "new spiritual and moral turn". What did he mean? Did this wish for a new direction express a conservative's longing to correct the seventies liberalisation of West German society by copying old ways? Was the intention to straighten out the anti-authoritarian features of this society, the features which had impressed me so much when I arrived and which had shaped me over the following years?

Chancellor Kohl reminded me of my friend Anton. Admittedly he was considerably older and fatter than Anton. He also spoke a completely different dialect. But he was a man of principle, with clear ideas of boundaries. He knew exactly who belonged here and who didn't, where the centre was in this country, and I was sure that he too had a gift for drawing straight lines.

I'm no longing sharing the desk with Anton but the country, Germany. Rather a funny idea. Anton and I are both Germans. I write poems, Anton writes computer software. I met him once by chance on the campus of Munich university. We instantly recognized each other and had a cup of coffee together.

Anton had turned into a smart young man who lived for his career without forgoing life's pleasures. I liked him.

"You were right," I found myself saying. "One needs boundaries in order to cope."

I don't know why I said it like that. Anton looked at me, baffled.

"I'm thinking about the boundary you drew on our desk."

He remembered nothing. And I didn't feel like telling him the whole story again.

I have been commissioned to write about Moslem prayer-houses in Berlin. In recent years these houses, whose members once would not even acknowledge one another on the street, have joined to form a circle. "Pull together on the rope of God, don't be strangled by the rope of the unbelievers," is the maxim on one of the flyers laid out at the entrance. Unique to slogans is the power to unite people whose thinking divides them.

I have decided to visit one of the prayer-houses in my part of town, one I used to know. It is a Friday, lots of people there. Men, mostly bearded, in shirt sleeves and bare feet. There is a queue outside the limited number of washrooms. The ritual wash always fascinated me. One washes, but cleanliness is irrelevant. Every child's dream. Turning the bathtub into a playground, one leaves dirtier than when one arrived. The ritual is brief. A few splashes onto one's neighbour's shirt, an especially loud clearing of the nose and mouth, is all there is in the way of tribute to the play instinct.

Islam seems to be the perfect community of faith for men who spend their whole lives producing nothing but foot odour, facial hair and sperm. The worst thing about this faith is that it proclaims purity where there is nothing but dirt. But what religion has ever succeeded in cleansing human beings?

In the course of my research I find all kinds of flyers with no explicit source. I don't know how to use them or whether I can.

The main work of our Holy Father is called Words.

A godless philosopher from France has also published a work with this title.

This is no coincidence.

God's Providence leaves no place for coincidences.

Undoubtedly this godless man knew the work of our Holy Father and deliberately stole His title in order to besmirch His Holy name.

By doing this he has condemned his work to death.

We must destroy the work of the godless wherever we find it.

In order that only the one true version of Words shall show men the way to happiness until the end of days.

The circle has published an address list of Berlin prayer-houses. It contains a total of 265 addresses. The list reminds me of a list of hotels from a tourist information office. From top to bottom on the left-hand side it gives names with addresses and telephone numbers. The prayer-houses are mostly named after caliphs and sultans. The most popular is Mehmet II, called Fatih, that is, the Conquerer. He conquered Constantinople for the Turks. On each horizontal line are entries describing the house's capacity, opening times, believers' mother tongues, language of the imam's Friday sermon, and leisure facilities – above all table tennis, body-building equipment, table football – which are usually in the cellar. "In the big city, traditional prayer-houses have become institutions of sociability," is how I conclude my article. "They are at once Moslem places and German social clubs. They claim their place at the centre of this society." Three days later the article appears as a full-page feature, not with my own title: "Friday Prayers, Sunday Ping-pong," but beneath the headline: "Moslems: a Threat to Civic Life?" The photo chosen to illustrate my article, to my surprise, is the golden dome of the recently renovated synagogue in Oranienburger Strasse.

27

For some time I have been thinking about the Cyrillic script in grandfather's notebooks. Grandfather knew Russian. He must have learned the language at school. The Russians had occupied some provinces in north eastern Turkey, including the city my grandfather came from, in 1877, and had set about civilizing the region straight away. Schools and administrative buildings were erected. These buildings even had central heating. My father could not remember ever having heard his father speak Russian. In general Turks are proud of knowing a foreign language. But Russian then was not what English is today. It was not a world language but the language of the occupiers. What then is the meaning of the Cyrillic script in my grandfather's most personal writings?

I go to Alex. He's a Slavonic languages specialist who translates the works of young eastern European writers. He can't read the Arabic script but he can the Cyrillic. So I can be sure that he can't read all of grandfather's writings.

I take the 1916 notebook with me, which contains a long passage in Cyrillic. Alex lives in an unrenovated old building in Prenzlauer Berg. It takes me half an hour in the tram to get there. I still cannot believe that this world is only half an hour away, rather than forty years. Up six flights of stairs. The stairwell smells of old frying fat and floor polish. I knock on Alex's door. Alex greets me, in a bad mood. He shows me a letter he has just received. The house has been returned to its old owner, who wants to renovate it. Modern loft apartments are planned, which will be accessed by an exterior lift. Estimated rent: 18 DM per square meter. Alex is still paying 4.50 DM.

"I'll have to find a different job or a different flat," he says bad-temperedly. "Or else I'll give it all up and travel the country going from friend to friend. Lots of people have a spare room or go away on holiday. I could get by as a bed-hopper." Alex has made strong coffee. "Show me the artwork." I hand him the notebook. He is the first person I have given it to. Outside, the weather has changed. A storm is attacking the roof. Individual drops are louder than the background music, Dvořák's Slavonic dances. He studies the notebook with lively interest. His tense features relax. "I can't read Arabic by the way," he says without looking up. I open a page of Cyrillic script for him. Alex reads out a short passage in Russian. Then he says nothing for a moment, looking at me. "That's from Anna Karenina, a quote from Anna Karenina, the beginning of the book." He goes over to a bookcase and takes down a German edition of the novel. "All happy families are alike, but every unhappy one is unhappy in its own way," he quotes from it.

I've never read the book but I know the quote from a different context. Isn't it quoted in another novel? When I leave Alex's flat I have some of grandfather's quotes in my head. All of them are extracts from the works of Russian masters, Tolstoy, Gogol, Dostoevsky. I have never liked the Russians. They bore me. I never even started Tolstoy. I can only ever get halfway through Dostoevsky's novels. The only exception is "Crime and Punishment", a work I'd prefer to any detective novel. But who had quoted "Anna Karenina"? I wanted to check back at home. I have four staple authors, it has to be one of them. Could it be Hemingway? If it was him, I'd surely have got it at once. For I know his works very well. It couldn't possibly be Kafka, or could it? Maybe Borges? Or Nabokov?

I suspected it was Nabokov's "Ada". Back at home I found that the book was missing. I must have lent it and not got it back. One rarely gets back books one lends.

Visiting Alex had calmed me and brought me a clarity I was no longer used to. The following day I took him all of grandfather's notebooks. Alex was to translate all the Cyrillic writing. "Give me one week," he said, "and I'll tell you more." I offered him a good fee and he agreed. That one week was not easy. It was the first time the notebooks had not been with me since I had been in the chancery in Munich. There was no reason for me to miss them. Besides, I still had the silver box, as I had taken the notebooks to Alex in three shoe-boxes. But the empty silver box intensified the feeling of being without the notebooks.

A week later I was standing outside Alex's door, full of excitement. I rushed inside when the door opened. "I've only been partially successful," he said quietly. "What's that mean?" I asked, worried. "Your grandfather was a charlatan. Not only did he incompletely reproduce the great Russian writers, sometimes he also wrote Turkish using Cyrillic letters. I can read that, but I can't understand it. I've rung a friend of mine who knows both Slavonic and Oriental languages. Sven speaks seven languages and understands a few more besides. He's the man you need. You can visit him now. He's expecting you today, since he's leaving tomorrow for a few days."

Now there was no going back. I was trapped. The Cyrillic characters in grandfather's text had taken away my fear about letting it out of my hands. But now I was facing the final deciphering. The language skills of a single person I knew nothing about might shed light on the darknesses in my origins. Did I want this? I no longer had a chance to ask myself this question. I set off for Charlottenburg immediately. The weather was sultry. In the Underground I found myself staring into the faces of people around me. They wouldn't be able to provide any information about me either. Besides, my story was a matter of complete indifference to them anyway.

All of a sudden Sven was to become a key figure in my life. But would he be able to help me? I could not make up my mind to cancel the appointment. So I was standing in his flat. It was a big, well-lit flat in an old building. "Let's go into my study," was his greeting. We went through a narrow hallway into a room at the end of the corridor. The room was almost empty. A chest-high desk stood in one corner. On it was a empty pad of paper. On the floor was a small pile of reference works. "I always work standing up," said Sven. "We can go and sit down in the kitchen once we've reached an agreement." Sven was the same age as me, blonde, tall and slim. He had short hair and wire-framed glasses. His three-day beard just about hid some scratches on his thin, bony face. He spoke flawless German. I held out the shoe-boxes like something nasty I wanted to get rid of. "I need you to translate all of it," I said. "All of it, as quickly as you can."

Sven put the boxes down on the floor side by side. He picked up one of the notebooks and opened it.

"It's going to take a while," he said matter-of-factly. "It's all handwritten, using an old-fashioned pen and ink, quite badly faded in places, the writing's not always very clear. If you want a good translation you'll need to be patient. This is a job that'll take at least a year. Have you ever worked with a translator before? A good translator only sees the text, nothing else interests him. So don't start telling me your stories. In my eyes these books are your story. Perhaps you already know what's in these books and you just want to hear my version. Any translation is always just a version. So you needn't explain anything. The best thing will be if you come here once a week and take part of the work away with you. If you have any questions meanwhile, don't ring me. I never answer the phone anyway. Keep your questions for your next visit. I'll invoice you for 500 DM for each instalment. We'll work out the final bill at the end, on the basis of 40 DM per page of manuscript." As a train roared past his house on the overhead line, drowning out his voice for a couple of moments, I realised I'd hardly been listening to him. I agreed to everything. All I wanted was to get out of his flat as fast as possible. Sven's brusque manner was what I wanted. He was at once direct and impersonal. He gave me the feeling of still being alone with the notebooks. His suggestion of coming to fetch an instalment a week was also just what I wanted. It would give my life a structure. Structures create meaning and contain fear.

30

In the entrance hall of my house a pin-board appeared last weekend next to the house rules. One of those brown boards meant for notes to remind oneself of things left undone. On it, a debate is being conducted about Germany. Apparently some people feel uncomfortable in our house. It is not enough for them to stand for hours holding up candles in the freezing cold in order to demonstrate for foreigners' right to life. Humanity cannot only be demonstrated in silence, it must also be demonstrated in language. Germany makes one writer puke, another is reminded of 1933 and asks whether there are any Jews living in the house. He offers them his protection come what may. And he would be very glad to meet them and develop human contact with them. I think about outing myself in order to meet him, but then I don't.

A few days later a new little note is pinned above the others, written in red felt tip: Please contact Dr Ferdinand Löbko, neuropathist, Monumentenstr. 14, Tel. 788 41 93.

At some point all the notes are lying on the floor and the caretaker sweeps them up and gets rid of them. Calm has returned to the house. I feel comfortable in Marie's flat in the back courtyard. She is away, but she always asks the right questions, which I am then unable to answer. Does one only ask oneself questions in case the answers help one prove to oneself that one is alive? Little of the sky can be seen from the ground-floor flat. Now and then one hears someone upstairs playing an accordion and singing. I like his songs.

31

Why the Turks came to Germany:

To work and earn money, to deal in drugs, to open a grocery store, to teach the Germans how to cook, to fornicate, to practise blood vengeance despite the cool climate, to learn the Koran by heart, to forget a woman, to recruit for the Turks, that suffering people, a football trainer and a Führer …

… and as they were standing at the border, a grey wolf appeared to them. It was a wolf in a grey uniform. A Herr Wolf. They worshipped Herr Wolf because he explained the way to Wolfsburg, after he had checked their passports. They all moved a little closer together and admired Herr Wolf's graceful manner in his grey uniform. Now they were surer than ever that in this country they would find a worthy Führer for that suffering people, the Turks. He would transform their country into a blossoming landscape in the shortest time. He would build houses and furniture out of the bones of the good-for-nothings, in order to make life better still for those who were hard-working and righteous. They were going to work hard in Germany and return to their homeland with an exemplary Führer at their head.

The first guest-workers – they came from Italy and Greece – were accommodated in the rotting barracks of the concentration camp in Dachau. There they were among themselves. They were not even unhappy. For they were beginning to fill their pockets with hard German marks. What more should Germany have offered them than money and fellowship?

32

The Germans don't like being imitated. They think people are making fun of them. It never occurs to them that people might imitate them out of admiration. Or simply out of not wanting to be different from them. Even if the others want to be like the Germans – the Germans' desire is to be completely different. They need their differentness in order to feel at home.

33

Maybe the reason why I have had no success as a writer is that I have not made enough of a display of my origins. I could have been interesting as a bilingual writer. But I am not bilingual. I could have been a Jew, with a descendant's direct line to the Holocaust. But nor am I properly that. Even if my mother was a German Jewess.

Am I a German? The question had never interested me. It hardly seemed to interest anybody. The question of German identity was an old-fashioned question, a topic laden with stereotypes and prejudices, a kind of rhetorical question, one that every rational person knows to evade with a gesture indicating insignificance. I was born in Munich. So I was a Münchener. Moreover I loved that city, something I could never openly admit to anyone in Berlin, as this would have amounted to a faux pas, making me an outsider instantly. I loved that narrow-minded bourgeois city, precisely because of its compact tidiness. I felt there as if my life was thoroughly planned out, nothing unexpected could happen to me. There, even the expected could not really affect one.

But something had palpably changed in Berlin with the opening of the Wall. It was as if the disappearance of the Wall had removed a protective skin which served as protection from the unknown in all its guises. The unknown that lurks behind the next corner feels more foreign and threatening than any fantasy involving someone exotic. The exotics who survived colonial history were domesticated by advertising. Advertising still carries on working like a magic formula to sever its objects from all reality. So the most alien things seem part of ourselves, without belonging to our world. Berlin was now a city open on all sides. It can be very windy in this city because there are no mountains far and wide. To the east the flat land goes on for thousands of kilometers until the Urals. Berlin is a city that is open to the east. But instead of being concerned with questions of meteorology, with the new and increasingly powerful winds, people in the city are concerned with themselves. This concern, which is an unremunerative but apparently existentially essential art-form, includes the question of who one is.

"Are you a foreigner?" I was asked whenever I spelled out my surname. Previously I had spelled it out without this question. Sure, according to my passport I was German. But that only complicated matters. Someone like me actually could not be a German at all. I had faced an elaborate naturalization procedure when I reached the age of eighteen. That was in 1972. Munich was hosting the Olympic Games. People in the city were international. In the police headquarters in Ettstrasse I sat sweating over a dictation. At that time a dictation was part of the naturalization procedure. It made no difference that one had been born in Munich, would take school leaving exams in a year, or wrote poems in the language that the official responsible for carrying out the test – due to a speech defect or his dialect – had considerable difficulties reading aloud. I do not know how many mistakes counted as failure. That was down to the official's judgment. Almost everything was down to the official's judgment. I made no mistakes. I was congratulated on achieving German citizenship. My mother had been born a German citizen, until her citizenship was revoked because of her Jewish origins. But I was given citizenship despite my Turkish father. I felt like a legal loophole, slashed into the ancient fabric of the German forest by the merciless and wilful machete of history. I had soon forgotten this unpleasant incident.

Now that the Wall has fallen and I am asked where I belong, it is all coming back. One never forgets, one represses. Just a single occasion, like the spelling-out of a foreign-sounding name, is enough to recall the repressed.

I have successful fellow-writers who are all good at remembering their origins. Remembering one's origins brings success. One has to distinguish oneself from the Germans in order to become visible.

How amazed I had been when my only literary publication, with the title *Veronika. Report on a Contemporary Love*, which had not enjoyed any reception for a long while – as one says when nobody talks about a book – was suddenly discovered within "foreigner literature". In academic accounts I was now a Turkish writer who used the German language with skill.

"Do you also write in Turkish?" I answered this question in all sorts of contradictory ways, just in order to confuse minds which were incapable of confusion. After all, who was to know that I hardly spoke a word of Turkish and was having to make an enormous effort to learn this complicated language, which obeys a logic entirely different from our Indo-Germanic languages. Colleagues of mine who were foreigners more visibly than I was, because they had dark skin or spoke German with an accent, seemed to have no problems at all with their reception as "foreigner-writers". They travelled around the country reading their texts at readings with other colleagues who were also foreigners. The audience that came to the readings consisted of Germans who wanted to see the foreigners. Somehow the whole thing seemed to have been planned in advance. A successful project. By now it was possible for a foreigner in Germany to trade as a writer with no more than a few texts laid out in the page so as to resemble poems. I was not interested. I boycotted all requests for interviews and turned down invitations to readings when other foreigners were invited, commenting tersely that I was not a foreigner, with the result that I won a reputation as a racist and xenophobe. Once an organiser referred to me as a "Möchtegern-Deutscher", a "would-be German". I liked the phrase. It solved my identity problems at a stroke. I liked puns too and my surname, Muhteshem, seemed to have inspired the man to make a pun which would never have occurred to me.

Meanwhile some Arabic and Turkish colleagues had discovered their forefathers' art of story-telling and were practising it in community college classrooms and other public places. Folk tales were in demand again. Folk story-tellers need animals to translate for them. The preferred animals in these texts were camels and above all donkeys. Since the animals in folk tales are generally cleverer than the people, the donkeys were always ready with a wise saying. One sensed that they had had to travel a long distance in order to address the German audience. The donkey-drivers were masters of their trade. They had expertly trained their animals for the visit to Alamania. The donkeys all spoke German, though a peculiar German, because what they said they did not think in German. German is a language that donkeys cannot think in. But they now served as proof that one need not think in a language in order to write in it. One can even extend the language by inventing words which one would never have invented if one had been capable of thinking in the language.

The Germans are a tolerant people. They let all this be done to their language. But then maybe by now their language has no value for them anyway. Or they find it just as ugly as they find themselves. At any rate they are more pleased about the visitors from the Arabian Nights than they are about the Gypsies in dirty clothes who come in over the green border by night and speak a single foreign word – "asylum" – in order to remain in Germany for the rest of their lives. Germany had become a country of story-tellers and petitioners, a country which no longer corresponded to my sober ideas, a country I had to leave.

I had gone to America. A country where a would-be German is left alone, as I had hoped. I had been glad to receive an invitation from the state with the fewest foreigners, the lowest quotient of immigrants. I had gone to the prairie.

34

Marie's return is delayed. That's fine by me. Her absence enables me to make progress with my own project, even if I am ultimately unable to say what this is. Is it not the fate of my generation to be working on projects which remain unnameable until their completion? And how often does it happen that they can never be completed, but remain endlessly self-ramifying fantasies which never let anyone seize hold of them? I cannot write a story until I know that the story belongs to me alone.

I am going to separate from Marie in order to be able to complete my own project. I am taking advantage of her absence to move out and get my belongings out of her flat. I do not know yet where I will take them. Several people I know have left town for a while and their flats are standing empty, but I instantly reject this idea. The flats are standing empty but they are not empty flats. They are full of objects and traces belonging to someone else. Someone left his life there before he went. He will come back and live there while I have to move on.

My life has left no traces. I must move into an empty flat and slowly fill it with my life. I have never yet lived in a flat of my own. In all the flats there were traces of other people, which I had to build into my life. My life became cumbersome. Maybe I'm sluggish. I get no pleasure from throwing things away, tidying up or moving the furniture around. This is how settled people renew themselves. They establish a new relationship to their surroundings and so protect their own deepest selves from major change.

I found that the idea of moving to the east of the city had a liberating effect. I was able to leave the city without moving away from it. I know some people think that the east is further away than America. It's not true. On the recently extended Underground line 2, it's only twenty minutes from Nollendorfplatz to Prenzlauer Berg. As a rule it's at least eight hours flight-time to America. What would that mean in terms of travelling time on the Underground, I wonder. When people say the east is further away than America, they must be talking about a feeling. That's one example of why I can make nothing of feelings. I do not agree that what one imagines must be accorded the same importance as what one experiences. Experiences contain enough imaginary already. More just cuts one off from life.

Alex had found work in Oriental Studies at the university in Frankfurt am Main. I had not been surprised. I never doubted his abilities. I moved into his flat. My only condition was that he had to leave it completely empty. Here in these rooms my life had taken a decisive turn. Here I had summoned the courage to confront what my grandfather had written. Here I could write again.

Meanwhile Marie was in Turkey, where she liked it so much that she extended her investigations in order to spend a few months there. I sent her a telegram. Her hotel had a fax machine of course, but I felt a telegram was more appropriate for Marie, apart from the fact that the effect is much more dramatic. I wrote: "Have moved out. All well." It cost me 12 marks and 15 pfennigs.

After returning to Berlin I had subscribed to a daily paper and I now cancelled the subscription. I felt at home in the new flat. I no longer needed a newspaper to orient myself. Instead I had my pad of paper and a pen on the breakfast table every morning. Now I could start writing my own news.

At last I feel in a position to tell the story as it happened. It might end something like this:

35

1936. The war was long since over, the country impoverished. He had been successful. He had not found it difficult to amass a fortune. The plundering had been good in the east. There was no chance that the owners of the abandoned properties could ever return. That had been taken care of. He had not expected that he would ever have to think about that past time again. Yesterday is yesterday, today is today, one tells oneself when one wants to forget what happened. In fact one could be proud of the past in this country. Even in the bitterest defeat one had remained steadfast, had never ceased to believe in ultimate victory. One had won. The price was high. But victories not won at a high price do not count. Real victories have nothing to do with gains. They are rich in losses.

He grew melancholy. He had loved her. But he did not know then what kind of feeling love was. He thought it was something that was not for him. He had to fight in order to kill, not in order to love. Life had had a meaning then.

He sits on the veranda of his summer house on the island. He is alone this weekend. He wants to write, he told them, urgent business letters.

When he received the letter a week ago he was surprised. He had not opened the letter immediately. He knew no one in France. There was no sender's name on the envelope. The stamp showed Pasteur, the discoverer, sitting at a microscope. It was not a long letter. Just a sign of life really.

The letter is from her. He trembles. The sudden memory of her overcomes him. She had remained the only woman he had loved. How had he been able to live without her all these years? How could he have children with a woman other than her?

"Our daughter knows nothing about you," she wrote, "though she's already twenty years old. She believes that her father is dead. Can it be that this is not true? Are you perhaps still alive and I do not know it? Had you not said that you would put an end to your life if we could no longer be together? One morning I was no longer beside you, and you are still alive? As I fled I was raped several times. Perhaps our child is not even

yours but belongs to one of the bastards, the traffickers and soldiers I met on the way."

That was twenty years ago. The past is coming to fetch him. He sweats. After the first reading he wants to burn the letter immediately. But he reads it again, and then again. He cannot answer it. She has not given an address and he does not know the name of the man she married. He would not answer the letter anyway. He knows what he has to do. She only wanted to remind him of his promise. A man keeps his promise, if he remembers it. He could also forget it. Would forgetting be a greater crime than the deed?

Evening is approaching. The din made by the cicadas is louder than usual. He loosens his tie, undoes the top button on his shirt. He has time enough. He will not be found for four or five days. He wants to die at night, looking at the stars. The sky will be my shroud. He grows melancholy. I'm getting old, he thinks to himself. "I'm getting old," he says to himself out loud. A cat which has come out for an evening prowl in the garden turns its head to look at him, then creeps on.

He loves the island. The quiet of the island. His wife and his son hate the island. "I can't stand this graveyard quiet," she says. "You can't hear nature," he rebukes her. "You're deaf from the city."

"I want to be buried here, in the garden of my house." The note he leaves is just this single sentence.

The funeral is a small affair.

Translator's Note

My thanks go to Professor Leslie A. Adelson, of Cornell University, for her detailed reading and precise critique of Şenocak's novel, and in particular of my translation (as it previously appeared online). See the chapter titled 'Genocide and Taboo' in her brilliant study, *The Turkish Turn in Contemporary German Literature: Toward a New Critical Grammar of Migration* (Palgrave Macmillan, 2000), pages 104–22 and especially the notes, pages 196–202. In revising I have often followed her suggestions.

Tom Cheesman

Swansea, May 2009

Hafan Books: *Out of Line* booklets

1. Million Gashaw Woldemariam, *Flight Safety*.

2. Humberto Gatica, *The Sand Garden / El Jardin de Arena*. Poems English/Spanish. Photographs by the author. Afterword by Nigel Jenkins. ISBN 978-0-9545147-5-4

3. Steve Short, *The Green Grounds and other ballads*. Afterword by M. Wynn Thomas. ISBN 978-0-9545147-7-8

4. Aimé Kongolo, *Reciprocities / Réciprocités*. Poems English/French. Drawings by Mary Hayman. Afterword by Sadhbh O'Dwyer. ISBN 978-0-9545147-8-5

5. Publication delayed due to the writer's fear of political reprisals against her family back in her home country.

6. Gemma June Howell, *Inside the Treacle Well*. Stories from the Welsh Valleys. Photographs by Chris Samia. Afterword by Karl Francis. ISBN 978-0-9545147-9-2

7. Alhaji Sheku Kamara, *Peace*. Poems / raps. Drawings by Mary Hayman. Afterword by Tom Cheesman and Sylvie Hoffmann. ISBN 978-0-9562409-2-7

8. Volker Braun, *What's Really Wanted*. Three stories, and *Shatter the Power Relations*, Büchner Prize Speech. Photographs by Eduardo Paca. ISBN 978-0-9562409-0-3

9. Zafer Şenocak, *Perilous Kinship*. Novel. ISBN 978-0-9562409-3-4

9B. Şenocak, *Perilous Kinship*. Conventional format edition (6"x9"). ISBN 978-0-9562409-4-1

Except 9B, format is 8.5"x11"

All proceeds to Swansea Bay Asylum Seekers Support Group

Online ordering at: **www.lulu.com/hafan**

Contact: **t.cheesman@swansea.ac.uk**